THE VENGEANCE OF LI-SIN

Jack Mallory steals a sacred idol from the temple of Tsao-Sun and brings it back to England. It contains priceless jewels, hidden by Chinese priests, and is booby-trapped to explode if tampered with. Meanwhile, Prince Li-Sin tries to kill Jack; a family friend, Dr. Hartley, saves him. But Jack will pay a heavy price for his theft. For both Hartley and Sir Edward Mallory have received the same threatening letter: 'The vengeance of Li-Sin will overtake you' . . .

Books by Nigel Vane
in the Linford Mystery Library:

THE VEILS OF DEATH
THE MENACE OF LI-SIN
THE MIDNIGHT MEN
THE VANISHING DEATH
THE DEVIL'S DOZEN

NIGEL VANE

THE VENGEANCE OF LI-SIN

Complete and Unabridged

LINFORD
Leicester

First published in Great Britain

First Linford Edition
published 2013

A catalogue record for this book is available
from the British Library.

ISBN 978–1–4448–1691–4

Published by
F. A. Thorpe (Publishing)
Anstey, Leicestershire

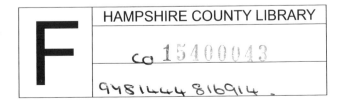

1

A Message From the Grave

The telephone bell in Dr. Hartley's quiet study in Harley Street rang shrilly. With a surprised glance at the clock, for it was past midnight, the doctor laid aside the book he was reading and, rising to his feet, went over to the instrument. Lifting the receiver he applied it to his ear.

'Hello?' he called. The deep tones of a man's voice came over the wire and he recognized it instantly. 'Why, Mallory,' he said, 'it's a long time since I heard from you. What's the idea of ringing up at this hour?'

'Sorry if I've disturbed you, Hartley,' said Sir Edward Mallory, 'but I rather want your advice. Some extraordinary things have been happening down here at Market Hailsham.'

'Extraordinary things? What things?' asked Dr. Hartley as his friend paused.

1

'I can't very well tell you over the 'phone,' was the answer, 'except that I believe that they are connected with that Black Idol business a year ago.'

Hartley started.

'In what way?' he asked.

'I don't know,' confessed Sir Edward. 'But I wish you'd come down. Jack and Jill are staying with me for a few weeks while their flat in town is being redecorated.'

Hartley's brows drew together in a frown as he considered before he replied.

'I'll run down tomorrow morning,' he said. 'Will that suit you?'

The voice that replied held a note of relief in its tone.

'It's very good of you, Hartley,' answered Sir Edward gratefully. 'Very good of you indeed. I hope it's not going to put you out at all?'

'A breath of country air will do me good,' replied the doctor. 'I'll be at Mallory Hall in time for lunch.'

He hung up the receiver, and going back to the fireplace filled and lit his pipe and stood smoking thoughtfully, gazing into the red embers.

Well he remembered the exciting events connected with the Black Idol a year before. Jack Mallory, during an exploring expedition, had stolen it from the temple of Tsao-Sun and brought it back with him to England. It was a hideous thing, but regarded by the Chinese as sacred. There had been a tremendous uproar in Tsao-Sun when the theft had been discovered. The idol was supposed to contain a quantity of valuable jewellery, which the priests had hidden there during a great rising of the people generations before. When these jewels were stored away inside they were embedded in a powerful explosive so that it was danger-ous for anyone to attempt to get at them unless they knew the secret of the idol. Prince Li-Sin, of the house of Tu-Lin, had followed Jack to England in an attempt to regain possession of the idol, and in the hall of High Hill, the house he had rented for the duration of his stay, had been blown to pieces together with the idol and Silverton, the crook, who had also been after it. A bullet from one of the detectives who had raided the house had struck the image and proved that the legend of the explosive was a true one. Memories of those exciting days welled into Hartley's mind as he stood gazing into the fire.

Jack Mallory had married Jill Marsh, the niece of Professor Arlington, who had been murdered because he possessed the secret of opening the idol. What had that telephone call from Sir Edward Mallory meant? What strange happenings in connection with the idol could be taking place at the little village of Market Hailsham? Li-Sin was dead. With his own eyes Hartley had seen the man blown to pieces, and yet apparently this midnight call had some connection with that year old affair, Mallory had said so.

He finished his pipe, tapped the ashes out into the grate, and went up to bed. It was a long time before he slept; his mind was too busily occupied in trying to conjecture what his friend could have meant. When he did eventually fall asleep his dreams were uneasy. A succession of sinister Chinamen were chased by a succession of black idols, round and round a circular room, watched by the huge figure of a crouching Buddha. Wilson, his manservant, bringing morning tea and letters, woke him unrefreshed. He drank his tea and turned to his correspondence.

There were several bills, two receipts, and a cheap-looking envelope addressed in printed characters. He stared at this wonderingly, and then, slitting it open, withdrew the single sheet of paper that it contained. Across it had been written, in the same printed characters as the envelope: 'The vengeance of Li-Sin will overtake you.'

Hartley read it twice with a puzzled frown. Who could have sent that message? Li-Sin was dead, so it couldn't have come from him. It must emanate from the Chinese group whose ruler he had been. Was this the explanation of Mallory's telephone call on the previous night? Perhaps he, too, had received something similar.

He shaved, bathed and dressed and went down to breakfast. Eric, his son, was already reading the paper, and to him Dr. Hartley showed the message he had received. The young man's eyes sparkled.

'I say, this looks exciting,' he remarked. 'Do you think these fellows could have popped up again after twelve months?'

'Looks remarkably like it,' said his father, and told him about Sir Edward Mallory's midnight call.

'It looks as if something interesting might happen,' said Eric. 'When do we go?'

'I've got one or two things to see to,' answered Hartley, 'but if you bring the car round about half-past ten I shall be ready.'

They reached Market Hailsham a little after twelve, swung into the chestnut drive of the rambling Tudor mansion that had been the home of the Mallorys for centuries, and drew noiselessly to a halt in front of the weather-beaten oak door. The grey-haired old butler, Rowson, emerged from the shadows of the hall and welcomed them, with a smile.

'Sir Edward is expecting you,' he said. 'It's a long time since we had the pleasure of seeing you, sir.'

'I've been rather busy,' answered Hartley, 'and the last time was rather exciting, eh, Rowson?'

The old butler's florid face became grave.

'Yes, sir, very,' he replied. 'Will you come this way, sir?'

He led the way across the huge hall with its suits of armour and dim coats of arms on the panelled walls and ushered them into the library. As they entered the large, lofty chamber Sir Edward Mallory rose from a chair by the fire.

'Come in, Hartley,' he said. 'Very glad to see you. It's extremely good of you to put yourself out like this.'

'Not at all,' answered Hartley. 'As a matter of fact I've been considering for several days looking you up. Well, what's the news?'

Mallory's handsome face clouded.

'The news is trouble,' he said briefly. 'At least, I'm afraid so. Sit down and have a cigar and I'll tell you all about it.'

Hartley helped himself from the box on

the table, and sank into a chair opposite his host,

'About a week ago,' began Sir Edward, 'I received a letter one morning addressed in printed characters and containing a single sheet of paper on which was written — '

' 'The vengeance of Li-Sin will overtake you',' broke in Dr. Hartley.

Sir Edward stared at him in astonishment.

'How the devil did you know that?' he asked.

'Because I received a similar letter myself this morning,' answered the doctor. 'But we'll talk about that presently. Go on.'

'Well,' said Mallory, 'I was surprised and rather startled, and then I thought that someone who knew about that Black Idol business was playing a practical joke, so I tore the thing up and threw it in the fire. Two days afterwards we had a scare in the village. Jill's maid, whom she brought down with her, had been out and was coming back after making some purchases for her mistress. She took the short cut across the common. It was a dark, misty night, and she was halfway along the footpath when two men suddenly sprang on her and pressed a chloroformed pad over her mouth. What might have happened we don't know, but luckily for the maid — her name's Teresa — Bland, the village constable, appeared on the scene at that moment and scared her attackers off. They ran like the wind and disappeared in the darkness of the night. But both Teresa and the constable swear that they were Chinamen! It puzzled me for some time why they should have attacked the maid, and then I remembered that she had been wearing a raincoat which Jill had given her.'

'H'm!' remarked Hartley. 'You mean you think they mistook her for your daughter-in-law?'

Mallory nodded.

'I'm sure of it,' he answered. 'Well, that was the first. The next thing that happened gave us all a scare, and inspired me to telephone you. The night before last Jack, and Jill and I were sitting reading in the drawing room. It was fairly late and we were all thinking of going to bed. It was Jack who made the first move. He had got up with a yawn and was announcing his intention of retiring when he suddenly stopped, staring at the window. I followed the direction of his glance and saw that a Chinaman was staring in at us, his face pressed close to the glass.'

Sir Edward Mallory paused, leaned forward and lowered his voice impressively.

'You'll think I'm mad, Hartley, but I recognized him. The man who was looking in at that window the night before last was Li-Sin, the man who was blown to pieces a year ago!'

2

The Death Call

Dr. Hartley stared at his friend incredulously.

'You must have been mistaken by a chance resemblance,' he said. 'It could not possibly have been Li-Sin. There is no doubt at all that the man was blown into a million pieces.'

Mallory looked at him queerly.

'I was not mistaken,' he affirmed. 'The man who was staring in at us through those windows was Li-Sin!'

'But it's impossible!' declared Hartley.

'Is anything impossible to the Chinese?' asked Mallory gravely. 'These people come from a long line of priests, Hartley, and the priests of Tsao-Sun are credited with being able to perform miracles, they are in close touch with the Lamas of Tibet.'

Hartley smiled.

'You don't believe all, that nonsense, surely?' he said. 'It would take a pretty hefty miracle to resuscitate Li-Sin after that explosion!'

'Well, I can only tell you what I saw,' said Mallory, quietly.

'Whether it was Li-Sin or not,' muttered Hartley frowning, 'there's obviously some devilry going on, and it's directed against us. The Black Idol caused enough trouble a year ago and apparently it hasn't finished yet.'

He broke off as a good-looking young man, followed by a pretty, fair-haired girl, came into the room. They had obviously just returned from a walk and their faces were glowing with the exercise and the frosty nip in the October air.

'Dr. Hartley!' said Jill Mallory in surprise as she caught sight of the doctor. 'I didn't expect to see you.'

'Neither did I,' said Jack, coming over and holding out his hand.

Evidently, thought Hartley, as he took it and returned the other's grip, Mallory had not mentioned his telephone message of the previous night.

'I thought I'd come along and see how marriage suited you,' he replied with a smile. 'Judging from your appearances it seems to suit you very well.'

Jill laughed, and a little flush crept into her face.

'It suits me all right,' she said. 'Did Father tell you that we are staying here for a few weeks while our flat in town is being redecorated?'

'So Sir Edward tells me,' answered Hartley.

'I hope you're going to stop,' put in Jack, 'we might have a go at the pheasants.'

'I shall be delighted to stop for a few days at any rate,' said the doctor, and thought privately that they might have a chance of going after bigger game than pheasants.

He had made no arrangements for staying, but had decided to do so on the spur of the moment after having heard Sir Edward's story. Mallory backed up his son's invitation, and Hartley arranged to send Eric back to town for the things they would need for their visit.

It was a jolly party that sat down to lunch in the huge old dining room, and although there might be a sinister and malignant agency at work against them it certainly failed to check their high spirits.

Eric left in the car immediately after the meal, arranging to get back in time for dinner, and during the afternoon Hartley, Mallory, and the two younger people, discussed the situation in the library.

'The trouble I started when I pinched that idol,' said Jack, 'seems to be endless, though I can't understand why these Chinese can't let the matter rest.'

'I can,' said Hartley gravely. 'They look upon us as directly responsible for the death of Prince Li-Sin, who was also a High Priest of the temple of Tsao-Sun. Through us, too, the sacred idol has been destroyed. They are under the impression that the gods are crying aloud for vengeance, and that untold disasters will happen unless that vengeance is satisfied.'

'Do you seriously think,' asked Jill, 'that we are in any danger?'

'I think we're all in considerable

danger,' answered the doctor. 'It would be absurd to attempt to make light of it. Everybody who was connected with that Black Idol business is in danger. We shall have to take very careful precautions, we are up against the ruthless cunning of generations, against the cleverest race in the world, a race who were civilised when we were savages, and who are familiar with secrets which we as yet have barely touched the fringe of. I strongly advise that from now on none of you go out after dark alone, the emissaries of Li-Sin and the temple of Tsao-Sun are obviously somewhere in the neighbourhood, waiting to strike. What has occurred is merely a preliminary. The attack will come suddenly, and without warning, and it will come in an unexpected way. By the way, is Inspector Parrish still here?'

Sir Edward nodded.

'Yes,' he answered. 'Though he's a Superintendent now.'

'Have you mentioned anything to him about the things that have happened?' asked the doctor.

Mallory shook his head.

'No,' he replied. 'Not about the man at the window, and the warning. The attack on the maid was, of course, reported in the ordinary way.'

'I think he ought to know,' said the doctor. 'I'll stroll along to the station and have a word with him.'

He enjoyed the walk through the crisp, frosty air, and arrived at the little rural station house just as the winter sun was setting.

Superintendent Parrish, larger and fatter than a year ago, was in his small office, and greeted Hartley with open-mouthed surprise.

'Well, this is an unexpected pleasure, sir,' he exclaimed rising with difficulty from his chair, and holding out a huge hand that was rather reminiscent of a leg of mutton. 'You've come down to see Sir Edward, I suppose?'

'Yes,' said Hartley. 'I'm spending a few days at Mallory Hall, and I thought I'd drop in and have a chat with you.'

'Very pleased to see you, sir,' said Parrish warmly. 'It's quite like old times to see you sitting there.'

16

'It's about old times that I want to talk to you,' said Hartley. 'I suppose you remember most of the details connected with that Black Idol business?'

'Remember them?' echoed the superintendent. 'I'm not likely to forget 'em, sir. It was that business that got me my promotion.'

'I don't think we've seen the last of it yet,' continued Hartley, and Parrish's prominent blue eyes opened wide.

'I don't quite get what you mean, sir,' he said.

'Well, I'll tell you,' answered the doctor, and drew his chair up nearer the desk.

Briefly and concisely he repeated what Mallory had told him that morning, and also acquainted the superintendent with the warning letter that he and Mallory had received.

'Sir Edward has destroyed his,' he concluded, 'but I've got mine here, I thought you might care to have a look at it.' He took the sheet of paper out of his wallet and handed it across the desk to Parrish.

The superintendent looked at it with interest.

'Well, you've certainly flabbergasted me, sir,' he said. 'I thought all that business was over and done with. Of course, I had a report about the attack on Mrs. Mallory's maid, and there was some mention of Chinamen, but I didn't really take that part of it seriously. I thought it was just an ordinary attempt at robbery with violence.'

'I'm sure it was much more than that,' declared Hartley. 'I think the maid was mistaken for Mrs. Mallory herself, because she was wearing a coat that Mrs, Mallory had given her. I think it was the first move in this scheme of vengeance.'

The superintendent wrinkled his forehead.

'Well, if you're right, it looks as if we were going to have some more of those exciting times,' he remarked. 'Sir Edward must have been wrong though about that fellow he saw looking through the window, it can't have been Li-Sin, we know he's dead.'

'Sir Edward swears that it was,'

declared Hartley, 'but I'm inclined to agree with you. Though I think it's Li-Sin who is the inspirer of this plan to avenge his death and the destruction of the idol. I've told you all this, Parrish, because we may need your help. I think there are agencies at work in the neighbourhood dangerous to any one who was connected with that business a year ago. The focal point of the danger is at present Mallory Hall, but it wouldn't surprise me at all to discover that they intend to turn their attention to every one who was connected with that idol business, and that includes you!'

'Me?' cried the startled Parrish. 'D'you mean you think that I may be in danger?'

'Eventually, yes!' answered Hartley, and then, as the superintendent smiled, 'I mean it! I think they'll concentrate on the Mallorys first, then possibly me, and after that, you!'

Parrish was obviously a little sceptical.

'I think you're taking the matter too seriously, sir,' he said. 'They may try to put the wind up us all by writing these warnings, but I don't suppose they'll do anything serious. However, if I can help you in any way just you let me know. By the way, the old Moat House is occupied now, you know, the place where they got that feller Silverton and tortured him to make him tell 'em what 'e'd done with the idol. It's all been done up, and an American family have got it.'

The conversation drifted into normal channels, and presently Hartley took his leave.

He was in the middle of dressing for dinner when Rowson informed him that he was wanted on the telephone. Thinking it was Eric who had called him up about something or other Hartley slipped on a dressing gown and went down to the library, where the instrument stood on Sir Edward's desk.

The room was deserted, and picking up the receiver he called: 'Hello?'

A soft sibilant voice answered him.

'Is that Dr. Hartley?' it said.

'Yes,' answered Hartley. 'What is it?'

'We have your son, Doctor,' went on the soft voice. 'You will find your car unharmed at the crossroads outside the village, but your son you will not see again!'

Hartley's face went white and set.

'Who are you?' he asked, hoarsely.

'You should know me, Doctor,' answered the voice. 'I am Prince Li-Sin!'

3

The Writing on the Ground

With a face that suddenly seemed to have aged ten years Dr. Hartley turned away from the now silent instrument. There was no mistaking that soft, sibilant voice. Inexplicable as it seemed, it had been Li-Sin who had been speaking. And he had got Eric. This was the first move in the scheme of vengeance. Clasping his dressing gown round him the doctor went in search of Sir Edward Mallory. He found him in his dressing room, engaged in finishing tying his bow tie. Briefly Hartley explained the situation, and his friend's face showed his concern.

'My dear Hartley, this is terrible!' he said. 'Terrible! What are you going to do?'

'Find the car first,' said the doctor, 'and then get hold of Parrish.'

He hurried along to his own room and hastily finished dressing. As he emerged into the corridor he met Jack.

'The Governor's just told me what's happened,' said the young man gravely. 'I'll come along with you, Doctor, if you like.'

Hartley thanked him, and together they hurried down to the hall. Slipping into their hats and overcoats they passed out through the big door and walked swiftly down the drive.

The crossroads lay about a mile distant, a mile that to Hartley seemed endless, but at last they reached them, and as they came within sight saw a car drawn up to the side of the road, all its lights on. As they approached it the figure of a constable came into view, silhouetted against the glare of the headlamps.

'Hello, Officer!' greeted Hartley. 'How long have you been here?'

'I've just arrived,' said the constable suspiciously. 'Is this your car, sir?'

'It is,' snapped Hartley shortly.

'Well,' said the policeman, 'You've no right to have left it here unattended — '

'I didn't,' broke in the doctor. 'My son was driving it and I've every reason to believe that he has met with foul play. You take this note along to Superintendent Parrish.'

He took out his pocket book, scribbled a line hastily in the light of the car's lamp and handed it to the constable.

'I oughtn't really to leave,' began the man, but Hartley cut him short.

'You do as I tell you,' he ordered harshly. 'It'll be quite all right, I'm an old friend of the superintendent's.'

Rather reluctantly the policeman took his departure, and when he had gone Hartley examined the car. In the back were the two suitcases that Eric had gone up to town to fetch, but except that the car was empty and there was no sign of his son, there was nothing to show that anything had happened. From the door pocket of the driving seat he took out a powerful torch, and directing this on the roadway he began to make an examination of the ground in the vicinity of the motionless car, but the frosty surface of the road showed no traces whatever.

'I'm afraid we shan't do much good here,' he said to Jack, who was watching him anxiously. 'Not that I expected to learn much.'

In spite of his words his voice was disappointed.

'They probably took him away in a car of some kind,' said Jack, and Hartley nodded.

'Almost certain to,' he replied, but it's left no traces on this hard road, so we're practically helpless.'

He was still sweeping the light of his torch about and suddenly he uttered an exclamation and brought the beam to a standstill, focusing it on a spot near the edge of the road two yards away from the car.

'What is it?' asked Jack, as the doctor hurried over and bent down.

'Look!' said Hartley, and his voice was full of sudden elation. Scratched on the roadway were two words:

'Mill House . . . ' Jack Mallory frowned. 'How did they get there?' he muttered.

'I think it's obvious,' answered the doctor. 'Eric left them, to give a clue to the place he had been taken to. They must have laid him down for a moment or two before they transferred him to the other car, and he managed to scratch this message with his nail.'

'The only Mill House that I know,' said Jack, 'is two miles from here. It hasn't been inhabited for years, and it's practically falling down.'

'That's the place,' said Hartley. 'These Chinese devils have probably been making it their headquarters. Which is the quickest way to get to it?'

Jack explained, and Hartley extinguished the torch and thrust it into his overcoat pocket.

'You wait here for Parrish,' he said, 'and tell him what's happened. I'm going along to the Mill House.'

'You'd better be careful,' warned Jack. 'Don't you think it would be advisable to wait until Parrish comes and let us all go together?'

The doctor shook his head.

'I'm afraid of the delay,' he answered. 'Even as it is I may be too late. No, I'll go along by myself, and you can get hold of Parrish and follow. I'll take the car to save time.'

He climbed into the driving seat, started the engine, and with a word of farewell to Mallory skilfully backed the car in the narrow road and turned it. A moment later he was speeding through the darkness in the direction of the Mill House. Jack's directions had been very clear, but even with them fresh in his mind he had some difficulty in finding the place. It stood on the slope of a hill, backed by a straggling wood, and surrounded by gorse bushes. The wreckage of its gaunt sweeps was just visible against the dark sky; the wooden structure of the mill itself was falling to pieces.

No light showed anywhere as Hartley made his way cautiously towards it. He had left the car at the edge of the road, and proceeded on the last part of his journey on foot.

The mill was sited in the midst of a waste of common land. A wild and deserted spot, eminently suitable for the emissaries of Li-Sin, if this was really their headquarters. But at first sight the place looked deserted. It seemed impossible that there could be anybody there at all, for it was so dilapidated that any light would have been visible in a dozen places. Hartley crept nearer, until the towering bulk of the mill rose almost above him. He could hear the creaking of the sweeps, the rattling of the slats as the wind blew fitfully, but although he listened intently there was no other sound.

The wooden structure was built on a brick foundation, and hugging this he began to make a circuit of the building.

He came presently to what had once evidently been the main entrance. In the days of the mill's prosperity it had been guarded by a heavy wooden door, but all that remained of this were a few baulks of timber and some rotting planks that hung drunkenly on rusty hinges.

The interior was dark, and cautiously he peered in. He could neither see nor hear anything, and his heart sank, Perhaps Eric's strategy had been detected; perhaps they had seen what he had written on the road and taken him somewhere else. A moment's thought, however, convinced him that it would have been far easier for them to have rubbed out the message, than to have gone to all this trouble. Much more likely the boy had not heard aright. Perhaps he had mistaken Mill House for something else. Certainly there seemed to be no one about here. However, it was just as well to make thoroughly sure, and Hartley cautiously entered.

The darkness was so complete that he couldn't see an inch before his eyes, and he had to feel every step before advancing. When he imagined that he had reached the centre of the lower chamber he stopped and listened again. Dead silence! Nothing but the creaking and cracking of the woodwork above him, and the faint whistle of the wind as it blew through the gaping chinks in the wall.

His fingers closed round the shiny barrel of the torch in his pocket and for a moment he hesitated. Then, deciding to risk it, he drew it out and pressed the button. The blinding light made him blink after the intense darkness, and then he saw that he was standing in a circular chamber, which had apparently been a storeroom. Several rotting packing cases were piled round the wall. In one place was a heap of decayed sacks, through the split sides of which had trickled little streams of mildewed corn.

Suddenly he heard a sound and stiffened. There came the hurried scurrying of tiny feet, followed by several squeaks, and he relaxed his rigid pose and smiled. He had disturbed the myriads of rats with which the place must be overrun.

Over on the far side was a wooden stairway, leading apparently to the rest of the mill, and going over to this Hartley mounted it cautiously. At every step he expected the rotten wood to give way beneath his feet but it held. He passed up through a square aperture, beyond which was darkness, and silence. Directing the light before him the doctor continued to climb. His head and shoulders had just emerged above the floor level when he saw in the light of the torch a malignant, yellow face peering out of the darkness within a foot of his own.

Startled, he ducked sharply, but he was too late! Something whistled through the air and struck him a heavy blow behind the ear. With a smothered cry he staggered, the torch flew from his hand, and losing his balance he slithered down the wooden stairway, to lie, a crumpled heap, at the foot!

4

The Man Who Was Dead

When Eric left Harley Street to return to Mallory Hall with the things he and his father needed for their visit he had no premonition of what lay in store for him before he had completed his journey.

London was swathed in a yellow fog, and this necessitated all his attention being concentrated on driving the car. Once clear of the suburbs, however, this lifted, and he was able to think about the strange business that had taken them to Market Hailsham.

In spite of Sir Edward Mallory's assertion that the face he had seen peering in through the library window was the face of the dead Li-Sin, Eric was inclined to be sceptical. There was no doubt that that sinister Chinaman was dead, and he was no believer in ghosts and such-like phenomena. It may have been a Chinaman that Sir Edward had seen, but it certainly wasn't Li-Sin. If a scheme of vengeance had been hatched against the people connected with the affair of the Black Idol then it emanated from some other source altogether. When that ugly and unlucky image had been destroyed, the explosion had been so terrific that scarcely a trace of Silverton or the Chinaman had been found. The hall at High Hill had been entirely destroyed, and Eric came to the conclusion that all the resources of Chinese magic would not be able to bring to life a man who had been practically blown to dust. An old nursery rhyme came into his mind and he chuckled as he sent the big car speeding through the night:

'All the King's horses, and all the
    King's men,
Couldn't put Humpty together
    again.'

And neither could all the priests of the temple of Tsao-Sun successfully put Li-Sin together again. That was an obvious impossibility; therefore, Sir Edward Mallory had been mistaken. Not that it really made much difference. Obviously, someone was at work, and whether it was Li-Sin or Chung-Li, or Wun-Lun, or anybody with the thousand and one peculiar names possessed by Chinamen, it came to the same thing.

Approaching the crossroads just by Market Hailsham Eric slowed up as he saw a row of red lights in front of him. Apparently the road was closed, which was funny. There had been no sign of any repairs or anything when he had passed this way earlier in the afternoon. Probably the local council had had an attack of energy in the meanwhile. The lights of his car showed him two trestles and a scaffold pole from which the red lights hung, and he brought the machine to a standstill with an exclamation of disgust. The only other way of reaching Mallory Hall meant a wide detour. He jumped down from the driving seat. So far as he could see there was no sign of the road being up. Probably this barrier was merely a preliminary warning, the actual excavations being some distance ahead. Still, it was funny there being no other lights to be seen. However, the barricade stretched from one side of the road to the other, and apparently, it was impossible to proceed any farther that way. There was nothing for it but to turn the car and take the longer way round to Mallory Hall.

He was in the act of going back to climb once more into the driving seat when two figures sprang at him from behind the shelter of the stationary car, and before he had recovered from his surprise sufficiently to offer any resistance his arms were gripped jerked behind his back, and swiftly tied.

'What the devil — ' he began angrily, but a third figure had loomed out of the gloom and as he opened his mouth to speak a gag was thrust into it and deftly secured by a handkerchief knotted round his head.

He was flung roughly to the ground and his ankles bound together, and then as one of his captors passed into the light of the headlamps he saw that he was a Chinaman!

Eric was by no means lacking in courage, but this discovery sent a little thrill of alarm through him. So the red light and the barricade had been a trap, put there with the object of stopping the car so that this attack could be made on him.

A fourth figure, tall and thin and clad in a heavy overcoat and a soft felt hat, rapped out an order. The three figures who had secured him hurried to the barricade, and swiftly began to dismantle it. The red lights were extinguished, the two trestles laid together and the scaffold pole which had rested on them flung over the hedge at the side of the road. A car, which he had not seen before because it had been standing without lights a hundred yards further down the road, crawled slowly up, and the lanterns and trestles were bundled into the back.

'Leave the car,' said the tall figure in a sibilant whisper, 'and bring the boy to the Mill House.'

Eric thrilled as he heard that voice, for it was the voice of a man he knew to be dead, but in spite of his shock his brain was working rapidly. If they were going to leave the car someone would discover it. Was there any means by which he could leave a clue as to where he had been taken? His hands had been bound at the wrists, behind his back, but his fingers were free, and it suddenly sprang to his mind that he could scrawl his destination on the hard surface of the road.

He rolled gently on to his side, and with difficulty succeeded in carrying out his scheme.

He had barely finished when two of the little Chinamen came over, and picking him up carried him to the waiting car and flung him into the back.

The car sped away and Eric began to wonder what would happen to him when they reached their destination. He had little doubt that whatever it was it would be unpleasant. He remembered something of Li-Sin's 'pleasantries' and in spite of himself he shivered. A quick death would not be so difficult to face, but that was almost too good to hope for. Undoubtedly something decidedly painful and lingering had been prepared for him.

The journey was a short one, for it seemed as though they had scarcely started before they stopped again. The car was brought to a halt at the side of the road and the occupants got out. Eric was hoisted from his uncomfortable position on the top of the trestles and carried across a waste of uneven ground, dotted with gorse bushes and trees.

He could see very little except the dark vault of the sky, for the arms of the man who held his shoulders prevented him turning his head. Presently, however, he was set down, none too gently, and looking about discovered that he had been laid in the shadow of a tall building that at first glance rather resembled a lighthouse set in the middle of dry land, but which a second inspection showed him had once been a windmill. So this was the old Mill House!

The two men who had been carrying him chattered together in Chinese, a language that Eric did not understand, and presently picked him up. He expected that they were going to carry him into the windmill, but apparently he was wrong for they skirted the brick base of the building and went on, up the slope until they came to the fringe of a belt of trees.

The trees concealed a long, low rambling building which was apparently the place they were making for, for they paused under a broken porch, dropped Eric again, and tapped lightly on the door. It was opened almost immediately and he was carried into a musty-smelling hall. There was no light and he could see nothing, and then, a door to his right opened and from it came a dim orange glow. He was carried into the room beyond and laid on a pile of silken cushions.

The pungent odour of burning Joss sticks filled his nostrils and he looked round, taking stock of his surroundings.

The walls and ceiling were hung with orange silk, heavily embroidered with green dragons. From the centre of the ceiling hung a silver lamp, burning perfumed oil and covered by a shade of orange silk. An orange and green carpet covered the floor and here and there were low tables on which stood several carvings in jade. Beyond these there was little furniture. A very low, ebony, inlaid chair and piles of green and yellow silk cushions. The curtains covering one wall had been draped back so that they formed a kind of alcove in which a big jade figure of Buddha sat placidly, and before which two golden sconces held lighted Joss sticks.

The two Chinamen who had brought Eric in bowed reverently to the seated figure of the god and then silently took their departure, closing the door behind them.

Eric lay back among the cushions and wondered what was going to happen next. He tested the bonds at his wrists and ankles, but they were unmovable, the material that formed them being some kind of hide. For a long time he stared at the tent-like canopy of the ceiling, and then a draught of cold air caused him to turn his head towards the door.

A tall, thin man, in a yellow robe, his hands hidden in his sleeves, entered slowly and pausing on the threshold stood looking at him.

'So,' he said, speaking softly, in a sibilant undertone. 'We meet again, Mr. Hartley?'

The newcomer was Li-Sin!

5

The Death of a Thousand Cuts

Dr. Hartley came to his senses to the accompaniment of a dull, throbbing pain in his head and a sensation of physical sickness. For some time he stared up into complete darkness, his dazed brain trying to account for these symptoms, and then, as the effects of the blow wore off he remembered: the malignant face of the Chinaman peering at him out of the darkness, the sudden agony in his head, and blackness.

He tried to stretch his cramped limbs and found that this was impossible. He could neither move his arms nor his legs and he discovered the reason for this when his groping fingers came in contact with the cords that bound them.

He was still in the old mill, he could tell that by the musty smell of decaying corn that came to his nostrils as he sniffed the air. Like a fool he had thrust his head into the lion's den and been bitten, and yet it had seemed impossible there could have been anyone in the place. He had heard no sound and seen no light. The man who had struck him down must have been aware of his presence and kept silent, waiting for just the opportunity which he had given him. There was one comfort, however, Parrish and Jack Mallory knew where he had gone and it wouldn't be long before they followed him.

The thought had barely entered his mind when he heard the sound of shuffling footsteps, and presently a dim light appeared at the entrance to the circular brick room, and he saw that it emanated from a lantern carried in the hands of a diminutive Chinaman. He was followed by another and coming forward they peered down at Hartley's prone figure.

'You come 'long with us,' said the bearer of the lantern in broken English. 'We takee you to His Exellency, Li-Sin, allee same great Prince.'

'Li-Sin is dead,' Dr. Hartley said steadily.

The wrinkled face of the little Chinaman became even more wrinkled as his thin lips widened in a grin that showed his yellow teeth.

'No possible kill Li-Sin,' be lisped. 'You see.'

He hung the lantern by a cord round his neck, and with a word to his companion stooped and took hold of Hartley's ankles. The other man lifted his shoulders and between them they carried him out of the mill and up the slope towards the belt of trees. When he saw the low building he realized why there had been no sign of life in the mill. This was the real retreat of his enemies, and he ought to have been sensible enough to suspect a house, for obviously the name 'Mill House' would not have referred to the mill itself.

He was carried across the hall, as Eric had been previously, and into the silk hung room with the orange light.

The first thing he saw was the bound figure of his son, and a throb of relief went through him when he saw that he was still alive, and apparently unharmed, and then he saw the tall figure in the yellow robe that was standing watching him. Something of his incredulity must have shown in his eyes for the expressionless face of the Chinaman altered and a faint smile lifted the corners of his mouth.

'You are surprised, Dr. Hartley?' said the soft voice. 'You did not expect that a man could survive such an ordeal as the explosion which destroyed the sacred Idol of Tsao-Sun?' He gave a jerky little bow as he spoke of the idol. 'You did not realize that a priest of the temple cannot die?'

'I did not,' answered Hartley, 'and I don't believe it now. There's some trickery, you are not Li-Sin.'

'Great and honourable doctor,' said the Chinaman, 'one of your greatest writers has said, 'There are more things in Heaven and Earth than the mind of man dreams of,' There are secrets known to China of which the white races have no knowledge. I am Prince Li-Sin of the house of Tu-Lin of Tsao-Sun, and if you wish for proof I can give it you. You remember how the man Silverton tried to force from me the whereabouts of the sacred Idol' — again he gave his little jerky bow — 'by placing the heating element of the electric stove across my chest?'

'Yes, I remember that,' said Hartley. 'What about it?'

The long yellow hands that had been hidden in the sleeves were withdrawn and the front of the silken robe pulled open.

'Look,' said the man who called himself Li-Sin simply.

For a moment that bizarre room seemed to swim before Hartley's eyes, for across the thin yellow chest ran a crisscross of scars. It was impossible, and yet without doubting the evidence of his own eyes he had to believe. There before him, alive and in the flesh, was the man whom he had seen blown into a myriad of pieces in the hall at High Hill a year ago!

'You are satisfied?' hissed Li-Sin.

'I am satisfied, but it's impossible,' muttered the doctor.

'Nothing is impossible in China,' retorted the other. 'In the mountains of Tibet are men living today who were old when the first steamship crossed the Atlantic. They possess the knowledge of light and darkness, the accumulated wisdom of the ages. They can heal the sick and raise the dead to life. Compared to theirs, my knowledge is as the wisdom of a child and its teacher.'

Hartley was silent His practical mind rebelled against the possibility of the things which the man before him implied. And yet he had read deeply and he knew the legend regarding the Lamas of Tibet.

'I have been given life,' went on the soft voice, 'because I have a duty to fulfil. The gods are crying aloud for vengeance against the desecration of their sacred property. I have been given life so that my hand shall be the instrument of that vengeance. Tonight the gods have smiled upon me, for, to use one of your English proverbs, 'I have killed two birds with one stone.' I never expected when I succeeded in kidnapping your son that I should so shortly have the pleasure of meeting you again.'

'Now that you've got us what are you going to do with us?' demanded Hartley.

'You will die,' answered Li-Sin calmly, 'as will all who raise their hands against the house of Tu-Lin and whose touch defiled the sacred Idol. I have in my mind three ways to kill you. There is the delirious joy of the 'Seven Gates,' or the exquisite pleasure of the 'Waters of Buddha', or the serene delight of 'The Death of a Thousand Cuts'.'

In spite of his evident control Hartley shuddered. Of all the ghastly tortures conceived by the ingenuity of the Chinese mind these were the worst. The doctor knew something about these subjects and his heart went cold.

'I see,' said Li-Sin, 'that you are acquainted with these methods for ensuring eternal sleep on the Terrace of the Night. I am glad, for you will then appreciate it the more when I tell you that of these three I have chosen for you and your son the 'Death of a Thousand Cuts';

the more familiar name, I think, is the 'Wire Jacket'.'

'You fiend!' cried Hartley hoarsely. 'You wouldn't subject either of us to that torture?'

'It is preferable,' said the Chinaman smoothly, 'to the 'Seven Gates'. I assure you that no one has ever withstood the raising of the fifth gate without going mad. It is less painful than the 'Waters of Buddha'.'

'If you intend to kill us,' said Hartley, 'why don't you shoot us and have done with it?'

The Chinaman shook his head slowly.

'To shoot you, doctor, that would be crude. I prefer something infinitely more subtle, more in keeping with the vengeance which the gods have decreed that I shall administer. To your Western mind the mere act of killing you would seem sufficient, but to we of the East who value life and death differently, it would be but a poor revenge. After all, what is death? A merciful release, an open gateway to the lands of eternal joy. No, the gods demand suffering, and you shall suffer twofold,

Dr. Hartley, for the first of you to wear the Wire Jacket shall be your son!'

He clapped his hands sharply and instantly three of the Chinamen appeared. To them he gave an order in the hissing dialect of his race. The yellow men bowed, two of them ran towards Eric, and the third took from a box that he carried a peculiar looking object that resembled a pullover, made of wire netting . . .

'It's monstrous!' rasped Dr. Hartley. 'You cannot do this thing!'

'I can and shall,' said the tall Chinaman. He lifted his arms above his head.

'Oh, God of Cathay, look down and bless the unworthy instrument of your commands!'

6

The Fight at the Mill

Left alone in the cold darkness at the crossroads Jack Mallory paced up and down impatiently. It was some time since Dr. Hartley had left him but as yet there was no sign of Parrish. Why in the world couldn't the superintendent get a move on? The doctor had insisted in going on to the Mill House alone and he wouldn't be able to put up much of a show against a horde of Chinese, and there was Eric, too. This delay might prove fatal for the boy.

Jack lit his fourth cigarette, puffed at it for a few moments spasmodically, and threw it away, as he had done the others. For the thousandth time he cursed himself for that foolhardy exploit at Tsao-Sun; if he had only left the damned idol alone all the trouble a year ago, then this echo of it would have been avoided.

Well, what was done was done. No use crying over spilt milk.

After what seemed an eternity he suddenly made out two dim lights coming along the road from the direction of Market Hailsham. This must be Parrish at last, He watched the lights as they covered the intervening distance, and then as they came nearer stepped into the roadway and held up his arms. There was a squeaking of brakes and the car came to a halt.

'That you, Mr. Mallory?' said the deep voice of Superintendent Parrish.

'That's me,' answered Jack. 'You've been an infernal time.'

'I wasn't at the station when the constable came back with the doctor's message,' said the superintendent, climbing laboriously out of the car. 'I'd gone home to have a bit of grub and they had to rouse me out. What's all the trouble, sir?'

As briefly as possible Jack told him. Parrish's thick lips screwed up into a whistle.

'Sounds pretty serious,' he said gravely.

'Dr. Hartley was round at the station this afternoon and told me that these Chinese fellers had popped up again. Well, they haven't wasted much time.'

'No,' snapped Jack. 'We seem to be doing that. Did you bring any men with you?'

Parrish shook his head.

'No, sir,' he replied. 'The doctor's message merely said come along at once.'

'Well, it's no good you and I going along to this Mill House place alone,' said Jack. 'We're neither of us armed and we don't know how many of these Chinese there may be. It will be worse than useless if we fall into their hands, too.'

'Yes, you're right,' agreed Parrish. 'The best thing we can do, sir, is to go back to the station, pick up three men and some arms, it'll only take a few minutes and it may be worth it in the long run.'

There was sound commonsense in what he said, and Jack, impatient as he was, agreed. He climbed into the car beside the superintendent and turning it, Parrish sent it spinning back along the road he had come. It took them five minutes at the station to collect the men and choose weapons from Parrish's little armoury. They were old-fashioned army revolvers for the most part, but capable of doing even more damage than their smaller and more modem prototype.

'We'll have to go carefully,' said the superintendent on their way back. 'We want to take these fellers by surprise if possible.'

Jack nodded.

Twenty minutes after they left the police station they came upon Hartley's car, standing where he had left it, by the side of the road. Parrish pulled his own car in behind it, and with a word to the three men in the back got out, followed by Jack.

They made their way cautiously across the uneven waste land and reached the base of the old windmill. There wasn't a sound anywhere except the moaning of the wind and the creaking of the old building, and halting near the circular brick base they held a consultation.

'The house proper,' whispered Parrish, 'is a hundred yards further up the slope.

That's where they'll be if they're any-where.' He turned to one of the men with him. 'You stop here, Davis,' he ordered. 'And if you see any sign of a Chinaman, shoot.'

The man nodded stolidly, and the superintendent, Jack and the other two men began to creep cautiously forward towards the belt of trees that surrounded the house. They reached it without seeing or hearing any one.

It lay in complete darkness, not a light showed in any of the windows, and when Parrish carefully tried the door found it fast and immovable.

'It doesn't look as if there was anyone here either,' he said in an almost inaudible whisper, with his lips close to Jack's ear.

'I think the best thing we can do is to make a circuit of the place, don't you, sir?'

Mallory agreed, and leaving the two men by the door the superintendent went to the right, while Jack went to the left.

They met again at the back in the shadow of some broken outbuildings.

'Not a sign of life,' began the superintendent and broke off sharply as from somewhere inside that dark and silent house came a muffled scream!

Jack heard it too and listened.

'There *is* somebody there,' he muttered, 'and there's devilish work going on too!'

The latter part of this sentence was spoken to empty air for Parrish, moving with surprising agility for one of his bulk, had disappeared round the angle of the house. Jack followed, and when he caught him up he was issuing hurried orders to the two men he had left by the front door. They stepped back a few paces, took a preliminary run and together hurled themselves against the blistered woodwork.

With a crash the door collapsed, and they stumbled into the darkness of the hall beyond. A high-pitched, excited chattering reached their ears, and two stabs of orange flame speared the blackness and were followed by the staccato explosions of a pistol. A bullet carried away Jack's hat and he heard another smack into the wall behind him. The growling roar of one of the army pistols crashed out an answer and was followed by a squeal of pain.

'This way, quick!' A muffled voice somewhere to their right reached their ears, and Parrish recognized the tone of Dr. Hartley.

He stumbled forward in the darkness and felt a thin body hurl itself against him and two claw-like hands clutch at his throat. He lashed out with the hand holding the pistol and it smashed into a face. There was a yell of agony and the clutch on his throat relaxed. He flung his attacker aside and continued on his way towards the place where he had heard Hartley's voice.

His groping fingers came in contact with a door handle, and grasping it he pushed but the door was locked. Stepping back he drove with the flat of his foot with all his force at the lock, and with a splintering crash the door burst open.

A flood of orange light streamed out from the door beyond and in it Parrish saw a sight that was to linger long after in his memory. Lying on a pile of cushions, securely bound, was Dr. Hartley, white faced and haggard. Eric, stripped to the waist, his body encased in a peculiar waistcoat-like arrangement of wire netting which had been drawn so tight that the flesh protruded through the mesh, was standing, held in the grip of two Chinamen. A tall, thin, yellow robed figure holding a gleaming sword was standing before the white-faced boy. There was blood on the sword and on the quivering body . . .

'Put up your hands, you devils!' shouted Parrish, his big face red with anger, and the tall Chinaman swung round.

His hands went slowly up above his head, and then, before the superintendent could guess his intention he suddenly slashed with the sword at the support of the hanging lamp. It cut through and the lamp fell extinguishing itself on the floor and plunging the room into utter darkness.

Parrish was afraid to fire for fear of hitting Eric, and then his ankles were gripped and he was jerked off his balance. He fell with a thud and the next moment was rolling over and over on the floor, fighting desperately with someone who was trying to strangle him.

From the direction of the hall came a terrific noise, thuds and groans and squeals of pain. Parrish succeeded in freeing himself from his adversary and scrambled to his feet. He stumbled over the door but in the pitch blackness outside he could see nothing. Fumbling in his pockets he took out a box of matches and striking one he held it above his head. In the feeble glimmer he saw Jack Mallory fighting desperately with one of the Chinamen. The little man was clinging to his adversary and succeeded in getting his hands round his throat. Parrish went quickly over and brought the butt of his pistol down on the Chinaman's head, and with a groan he relaxed his grip and rolled over on the floor.

'Thanks,' panted Jack, scrambling to his feet, and at that moment the match in the superintendent's hand burnt down to his fingers and went out.

The darkness only lasted for an instant, however, and then one of the constables switched on the powerful ray of an electric torch.

'By God, that was hot while it lasted, sir!' he grunted, and Parrish nodded.

The hall of the house was a shambles. The floor was slippery with blood. One of the policemen was groaning with a knife wound in the fleshy part of his arm. At the foot of the stairs a Chinaman lay unconscious, and huddled up against the wall in one corner another one dead. The superintendent gave a quick glance round, took the torch from the constable's hand, and went back into the room where he had last seen Eric and Dr. Hartley.

It was empty now, except for the doctor and the boy. Of the tall Chinaman there was no sign. He had left his sword behind on the floor and with this the superintendent cut the thongs binding the doctor.

'I'm all right,' grunted Hartley as he rubbed at his limbs to restore the circulation. 'Attend to Eric, will you?'

Jack went over to the boy and released

the screws that held the devilish wire arrangement round his body. The little knobs of flesh, which had protruded through the mesh had been cut in several places and he was bleeding profusely. The fantastic name of the 'Death of the thousand cuts' was no exaggeration. With the assistance of the doctor, who staggered over, Jack managed to staunch the blood and when they came to examine him they found that beyond a very painful experience no great damage had been done.

While they attended to Eric, Parrish collected his men and searched the building. It had obviously been the headquarters of the Chinese group, for in the upstairs rooms they found several mattresses and bed clothing. In the kitchen was a collection of dirty vessels, which had been used for cooking. The only room in which any attempt at furnishing had been made was the one with the yellow hangings. This had obviously been Li-Sin's sanctum.

From the number of mattresses the superintendent concluded that there must have been at least twelve occupants, and of these twelve they could only account for two: the dead man who had been killed by a bullet from one of the policemen's pistols and the wounded man. The rest had evidently succeeded in getting away.

Neither was there any trace of Li-Sin.

When Eric's wounds had been roughly dressed Parrish collected the wounded Chinaman, who was not seriously hurt, and leaving the house they made for the cars, and here a surprise awaited them, for of the two cars that had originally stood by the side of the road only one remained, the superintendent's police car, Dr. Hartley's had vanished!

'They took it to make their get-away in,' grunted the superintendent. 'Well, it may prove a means by which we can trace them.'

Hartley shook his head.

'Li-Sin's too clever for that,' he replied. 'They won't go very far in it, it'll be found abandoned somewhere.'

Parrish looked at his own car and made a grimace.

'Well, we shall have to go back in mine,' he said. 'Though it's going to be a tight squeeze, sir.'

It was a tight squeeze, but they managed to do it, and after dropping the constable and their prisoner at the police station the superintendent drove them on to Mallory Hall.

As they drew up at the big arched entrance Rowson appeared at the head of the steps and came down to meet them.

'Well, we've got back,' said Hartley cheerily, 'and not much damage has been done. Where's Sir Edward, Rowson?'

The butler looked at him and his lined old face expressed surprise.

'Haven't you seen him, sir?' he asked. 'He said he was going to the crossroads to find you.'

7

The Thing in the Car

'How long ago was this?' asked Hartley sharply.

'About half an hour ago, sir,' said Rowson.

'He must have missed us,' muttered Jack. 'Probably we passed him on the road.'

'We didn't pass anybody,' declared the doctor, and his face was worried. 'The road isn't very wide, and if we had we should have seen him in the light of the lamps.'

They went in to the big hall, and Jill came out of the drawing-room. At the sight of Eric's white face she gave a little gasp of alarm.

'Is he hurt?' she whispered, anxiously.

Jack shook his head.

'No, darling, he's all right, luckily,' he answered. 'We were in time.'

The girl gave a sigh of relief.

'Oh, I'm so glad,' she said. 'I've been terribly worried. It was because I was so worried that Father went out to follow you. Did you see him?'

Jack shook his head.

'No we missed him somehow,' he answered, and although he strove to speak lightly there was something in his voice that made her look at him quickly.

'But it's almost impossible you could have missed him,' she said. 'He left here half-an-hour ago on his way to the crossroads!'

'Perhaps,' suggested Superintendent Parrish, 'when Sir Edward got there, finding nobody about, he didn't wait.'

'In that case he'd have come back here,' said Hartley, 'and we should have caught him up. I don't like it, Parrish. I don't like it at all.'

The superintendent looked at him in surprise.

'Good Lord, sir!' he exclaimed. 'You don't think — '

'I think he's run foul of that Chinese devil,' said Hartley, through his teeth.

'They got away in my car, didn't they? Well, Mallory knows that car well. If he'd seen it on the road he'd have tried to stop it, and if Li-Sin and his crew of cut throats were on board they'd have recognized him and looked upon it as a heaven-sent opportunity.'

His listeners stared at him in horror.

'My God!' muttered Jack. 'It's awful!'

'In case you're right, sir,' said Parrish quickly, 'I'd better get back to the station and send out a hurry call with a description of the car to all stations. We may be able to get them that way.'

'It's worth trying,' said Hartley, but his tone was dubious. 'At the same time, Li-Sin is no fool and he'll guess that's the first thing you'll do. He'll stick to the car only so long as he considers it safe, then he'll find some other means of transport. If only we knew where he was making for! We've smashed up his hideout at the old Mill House, he can't go back there.'

'I expect he's got a dozen places he can go to,' said Jack. 'He's sure to have foreseen the possibility that he'd have to leave the Mill House in a hurry and prepared for the eventuality.'

Hartley nodded gloomily.

'Well, anyway, Parrish's scheme is worth trying,' he said.

'I'll get along now, sir,' said the superintendent, and bade them a hurried goodbye.

They heard his car go noisily down the drive, and Rowson closed the big front door.

In the general excitement dinner had been forgotten and now, although this fresh worry had come to them, they began to feel hungry. They were too upset, however, to sit down to a laid meal, and Jill ordered sandwiches and coffee to be brought to the drawing-room. Dr. Hartley ordered Eric to bed at once, and after vainly protesting against this parental edict, his son went.

There was just a bare chance that nothing had happened to Sir Edward Mallory, and they waited, hoping that he would return, but as the time slowly passed this hope decreased until at ten o'clock it had ebbed away to nothing. At half-past-ten the telephone bell rang. Dr.

Hartley answered the summons eagerly, hoping that it was some news. But it was only Superintendent Parrish calling to know if anything had been heard of Sir Edward. The doctor informed him that nothing had, and went back to the drawing-room.

Jack and Jill were very silent, afraid to put into words the thoughts that were worrying them. There could be little doubt now that something had happened to Sir Edward, for it was ridiculous to suppose that he had kept away so long of his own free will, and it seemed obvious that he must have fallen into the hands of Li-Sin. If he has, God knows what's happened to him, thought Dr. Hartley.

The Chinaman was probably furious at his plans having miscarried at the Mill House, and if he had succeeded in getting Mallory into his clutches it was possible that he would vent his spleen on the old man.

'Look here,' said Jack, suddenly stopping in his ceaseless pacing of the room, 'I can't stand doing nothing. If any news comes through Jill's here to answer the telephone. Suppose we go and have a look round? Father may have twisted his ankle or something. It may not be so serious as we imagine, and anyway, it's better than doing nothing.'

Hartley welcomed his suggestion with relief. Going out into the hall they struggled into their overcoats. 'Which way shall we go?' he asked as they set off down the drive.

'Let's walk up towards the crossroads,' suggested Jack 'You take one side of the road and I'll take the other.'

Hartley agreed, and they put this plan into execution, but they reached the crossroads without finding anything. They were not very disappointed. It had, after all, been only a forlorn hope. It was unlikely that Sir Edward had met with any accident, but the possibility had been worth taking into consideration, and acting upon.

They retraced their steps and near the entrance to the drive Jack suddenly touched Hartley on the arm.

'Look!' he said in wonder.

Following the direction of his gaze

Hartley saw, drawn up near the gates, a car. The lights were out and they might have missed it all together in the darkness of the night if it had not been for the fact that a cyclist coming towards them at that moment had shown it up dimly in the light of his lamp. They hurried towards it and one glance at the long radiator told Hartley that it was his own!

'Well, of all the audacious things!' he exclaimed. 'That devil must have brought it back and left it here.'

A cold hand clutched at Jack's heart.

'You don't think,' he said hoarsely, 'that anything's happened to Jill?'

The doctor started.

'My God! I hope not,' he said. 'You'd better hurry up to the house and see.'

Jack was on the point of hurrying away when Hartley saw something and called him sharply:

'Come here,' he said, and his voice was strained and unlike his own.

Mallory turned back.

'What is it?' he asked.

Hartley had opened the door leading to the driving seat and was peering into the interior. As Jack joined him he pointed silently.

'Look!' he said, in a low voice.

Jack looked, and saw, crouched over the wheel, a motionless figure.

'My God!' he said. 'Who is it?'

For answer Hartley switched on the dashboard light, and as it shed its rays on the white face and staring eyes he uttered a cry of horror.

'Good God! It's Father!' he exclaimed.

It was Sir Edward Mallory, and he was dead! Killed by the thin silk cord that had been tied tightly round his throat. Later they found pinned to the front of his overcoat a sheet of paper on which had been printed:

The Vengeance of Li-Sin has over-taken him!

8

A Scrap of Paper

The morning came coldly to a household shrouded in gloom. Upstairs in his bedroom, silent and motionless on the bed he had used in life, lay all that remained of Sir Edward Mallory.

Superintendent Parrish had been telephoned for immediately after the discovery, and had arrived with the police surgeon. Death had been due to strangulation, and the message that had been found on the body left no doubt as to who was responsible.

The servants went about their duties silent and red-eyed, for Mallory had been well loved, and his loss was keenly felt, both by his family and his retainers. Jill had been so overcome that on Jack's orders she had gone to bed and remained there. Hartley, Eric and the young man breakfasted together, a gloomy meal that was disturbed by the arrival of the superintendent.

'I'm going up, sir,' he announced, 'to have a look at the Mill House by daylight. It occurred to me early this morning that there might be some clue up there that we've overlooked, and I called in here, thinking perhaps you'd like to come with me.'

'I should,' said Hartley. 'If you'll wait while I finish this coffee we'll go along.'

'Perhaps you'd like one too?' said Jack and Parrish thanked him gratefully.

'I would, sir,' he answered. 'It's a cold morning.'

He had come in his car, and when they had finished their coffee they went out and climbed into the machine. Half an hour later they were standing once more at the entrance to the old Mill House.

In the light of day it looked even more gloomy and sinister than it had done the previous night. There was scarcely any glass in the windows, and the walls were cracked, and in places the roof had sagged. They entered by the shuttered front door and looked round the hall. The traces of the fight that had occurred there were still visible on the dusty boards. Parrish gave a hasty glance round and then made for the room with the silken hangings.

They found the window first and tore aside the silk to admit the light. The hangings looked rather tawdry when this was done, and it occurred to Dr. Hartley that the place was rather reminiscent of a fortune-teller's booth at a circus, although the silk was of the finest quality, and the carpet of a deep pile into which their feet sank noiselessly.

They made a thorough search of the place but found nothing that was likely to be helpful. There was another room on the ground floor, but this apparently had been unused, for the floor was inches deep in dust and there were no sign of any footprints.

'How about that wounded fellow?' asked Dr. Hartley, as they ascended the stairs, to continue their search on the upper floor. 'Can't you get something out of him?'

Parrish shrugged his shoulders.

'I've tried, sir,' he said, 'but he's as dumb as an oyster. Pretends he doesn't understand English, which may be true for all I know.'

'You should get Mr. Mallory to see him,' said the doctor, 'he speaks Chinese.'

'That's a very good idea, sir,' said the superintendent. 'I'll remember that.'

They started with the dormitory-like room containing the mattresses, where the Chinamen had ominously slept, and here, towards the end of their search, they made a discovery. It was a torn scrap of dirty paper and on it had been scrawled: 'Ho-Ling. R — '

It was Parrish who found it and he brought it over to Hartley.

'What do you make of this, sir?' he asked.

The doctor examined it.

'Nothing,' he replied. 'Looks to me as if it might be one of the feller's names.'

'Or an address, sir,' suggested the superintendent,

'If it is an address the address part has been torn off so it isn't much use. There must be thousands of Ho-Lings in

Liverpool and Limehouse, it's a very common Chinese name.'

Parrish grunted his disappointment.

'I thought we might have found a clue,' he said. 'Still I'll keep it, it may come in useful.'

He stowed it away in his wallet and they continued the search, but they found nothing else, and when they finally left the dilapidated house they were as wise as when they entered it.

Going back to Mallory Hall they found Jack raging up and down the library.

'Hello, what's the matter?' asked Hartley.

'This,' snapped the young man harshly. 'Read it.'

He thrust a letter into the doctor's hand, and Hartley read the carefully-printed writing. It started without preliminary:

'You may try but you cannot escape the vengeance of the gods. I, Li-Sin, who am their instrument, do swear humbly before my ancestors that no one bearing the name of Mallory shall escape my vengeance.'

'That came by the second post,' said Jack. 'By God! I'd like to have five minutes alone with that fellow Li-Sin!'

'Have you got the envelope, sir?' asked Parrish practically.

'Yes.' Jack went across to the big writing table and picked it up.

The superintendent took it from him and looked at it. It was of cheap quality and the postmark was Pennyfields.

'This was posted near Limehouse, sir,' he said, 'so I should say that's where he's gone to earth.'

'He'd go to earth in six feet of ground if I had my way,' snarled Jack.

Dr. Hartley had been frowning thoughtfully at the fire but looked round.

'Can I use your telephone?' he said.

Jack nodded.

The doctor went over to the instrument and lifted the receiver.

'Give me Whitehall 1212,' he said, and then while he waited for the connection to be made: 'I'm going to ring up Inspector Gladwin, you remember he helped us with the other business a year ago. He may be able to give us some information about that scrap of paper you found under the mattress.'

'I was going to ring up the Yard myself, sir,' said Parrish, 'when I got back to the station, but you go ahead.'

'Hello, Scotland Yard?' said Dr. Hartley turning to the instrument. 'Put me through to Inspector Gladwin, will you? Tell him it's Dr. Hartley, of Harley Street.' A few seconds later he heard the inspector's deep voice.

'Hello, Doctor,' said Gladwin. 'What can I do for you?'

Briefly Hartley explained what had occurred at Market Hailsham, and the inspector listened attentively.

'I'm sorry to hear about Sir Edward,' he said sympathetically when the doctor had finished. 'So those devils have sprung up again, have they? What was that name again?'

'Ho-Ling,' said Hartley.

'Ho-Ling?' He could almost see Gladwin's heavy face puckered up thoughtfully. 'I can't recall the name at the moment, but I'll tell you what I'll do, I'll get through to the divisional inspector of K division and ring you up in half-an-hour. If Ho-Ling refers to a place anywhere round Pennyfields he'll know it.'

Hartley thanked him and rang off.

'Well, that's something,' he remarked, 'but whether it will lead to anything or not, we can't tell.'

The atmosphere of gloom that had settled on the house had not lifted. It seemed that with the death of the master something about the bricks, and mortar and furnishings had died too. There was a tomb-like silence about the place, which is noticeable in any building where death has called, and claimed a victim. The servants moved softly about their work as though afraid to disturb the silent figure that lay shrouded by a sheet on the bed upstairs.

While they waited for Gladwin's telephone call they chatted in low voices, going over and over again in detail the tragedy that had happened, trying to evolve some plan of campaign, and completing the circle found themselves where they began. It was three-quarters-of-an-hour in fact before the telephone bell shrilled and Hartley picked up the instrument.

'Hello? Yes. Hartley speaking,' he said. 'Well? Oh, thanks, Gladwin. Yes, Just a moment,' He pulled a sheet of paper towards him and picked up a pencil. 'Go ahead,' he continued, and scribbled something as Gladwin spoke. 'I'll drop in and see you this afternoon,' he said, and hung up the receiver.

Turning, he read what he had written:

'Ho-Ling's — I don't know whether it's the same or not, of course — is a restaurant off Limehouse Causeway. Apparently it's quite a respectable place, but if that scrap of paper refers to it it's probably the present headquarters of Li-Sin.'

Parrish rubbed his hands.

'Well, that's something,' he said with satisfaction. 'I'd better get in touch with the superintendent of Limehouse division.'

'I'd rather you didn't, Parrish,' said Hartley. 'I don't think they can do any good. Li-Sin's clever and the first sign of a policeman around the place will keep him lying low, even if the police could discover anything, which I doubt. No, I've got a better plan. I shall go up to town this afternoon, see Gladwin and get all the information I can about this Ho-Ling, and then go along there myself tonight, and have a look round.'

Parrish's face expressed his disapproval.

'It's dangerous, Doctor,' he said. 'These Chinese know you well, and if they should recognise you — ' Instead of finishing the sentence he snapped his fingers.

'They won't recognise me,' said Hartley. 'You don't suppose I'm fool enough to go there as I am, do you? By the time I've finished I doubt if my own mother would recognise me.'

'I'll come with you,' said Jack, but the doctor shook his head.

'No, you won't,' he replied. 'You'll stop here, you've got Jill's safety to consider, you can't leave her alone.'

'No, that's true.' muttered the young man.

'But if you'll take my advice,' went on the doctor, 'you'll arrange with Parrish to have a guard put on the house. It's obvious from that letter that the present intention is to wipe out the Mallorys, and this is a lonely place and a hoard of Chinese could easily overcome you and Rowson and the two other male servants.'

'I'll have a man sent up,' said Parrish.

'One man's no good,' said Hartley. 'You'd better send up three, and they'd better be armed. I know the British policeman dislike carrying firearms, but when he's dealing with people like Li-Sin and his gang of villains it's just as well to take precautions. A truncheon's not much use against a knife or a pistol.' He crossed to the door. 'Well, I'll be off,' he said. 'Good luck until I come back.'

He collected Eric and going round to the garage brought out his car.

Inspector Gladwin greeted him with a smile when he was shown into his bare office, and motioned him to a seat.

'Well, I haven't seen you for a long time, Doctor,' he said. 'So these Li-Sin people have turned up again, have they?

Of course, it can't be Li-Sin.'

'I'm not so sure of that,' said Hartley. 'But whoever it is, he's just as dangerous and just as cunning. Now, tell me all you know about Ho-Ling.'

'It's quite a respectable place,' said the inspector, 'as those places go. He's suspected of running a dope parlour and being interested in a gambling establishment, but we've got no proof against him, and the place is very well conducted.'

'Is it the sort of place that Li-Sin would use for headquarters?' said Hartley.

Gladwin shrugged his broad shoulders.

'You can't tell with these Chinese,' he said. 'They hang together like Masons. I should say it was quite possible.'

'Well, I'm going there tonight,' said the doctor, and the inspector almost word for word repeated Parrish's warning.

'I don't think there'll be much risk,' said Hartley. 'I shall disguise myself carefully, but if I don't ring you up by eight o'clock tomorrow morning you'd better send someone to look for my body!'

He talked for a few moments longer

and then took his leave. The rest of the day he spent at Harley Street, resting in anticipation of his night's exertion. At seven o'clock he went up to his bedroom and produced a make-up box from the wardrobe. He had carefully considered the question of what disguise he should adopt and decided that according to Gladwin's description of the place a lighter-man would be appropriate. By nine o'clock he was ready to leave the house, a very different being to the immaculate Hartley who usually passed through that staid front door.

'Don't go out,' he warned his son, before taking his departure. 'I've told Wilson he's not to answer the door to anyone.'

Eric was obviously concerned for his father's safety, but Hartley had resolutely refused to listen to his entreaties that he should be allowed to come too.

He took a train to Aldgate and from thence travelled by motor-bus to Penny-fields. When he got off the bus he found himself within some ten minutes' walk of the place he was seeking, and set off at a brisk pace.

The front of Ho-Ling's was dingy enough; an ordinary rather second-rate Chinese restaurant. Hartley entered, found a table in a quiet corner and gave a light order to the Chinese waiter, and while the man had gone lit a cigarette and surveyed the place. Business was very quiet that evening apparently. There were only about three persons present, and two were celestials who were talking together in an absorbed way. And then a pair of heavy curtains that screened an archway at the far end of the room attracted his attention. Some movement of these had drawn him and he felt a curious sensation as though he was being watched. He turned his eyes away and carelessly took out his cigarette case, which, in accordance with his disguise, was a cheap one of chromium plate. In the polished surface he could see a clear reflection of the alcove, and as he looked, the curtains parted in the middle and a yellow face peered out. The almond shaped eyes staring straight at him.

He slipped the case back in his pocket and his heart was beating fast. There was no doubt that Ho-Ling's was the place that Li-Sin had made his temporary headquarters, for it was his face which the doctor had seen peering from between the folds of the heavy curtains!

9

The Invisible Death

Dr. Hartley ate the light meal that was brought him, his brain working rapidly, and his senses alert and watchful. It was useless his remaining in the restaurant part of the building. He would learn nothing that way. It was essential that he should see the more private part, and he racked his brain to think of a feasible scheme by which this project could be put into execution. What interested him most was what lay behind those heavy curtains. Apparently they formed no exit or entrance to the place, for he had watched closely and no one as yet had gone through them.

At the end of his meal, when the waiter came to remove the last dish he beckoned him. The Chinaman bent his face and Hartley whispered in his ear.

'Muchee want pipee,' he said. 'Allee

slame pay muchee money?'

The Chinaman shook his head.

'No smokee here,' he replied. 'This allee slame lespectable lestaurant.'

Obviously, thought Hartley, shrugging his shoulders, Ho-Ling was careful. Although Gladwin had stated that he ran a dope parlour it was evidently only open to known customers. No stray clients were admitted. He had hoped that subterfuge would lead him to see what lay beyond those curtains, but apparently it had failed.

He lit another cigarette, and had half smoked it when the Chinese waiter came gliding up to his side.

'How muchee pay smokee?' he asked.

'Anythin' within reason,' growled Hartley. 'I could do with a whiff.'

'You come 'long me,' said the waiter persuasively. 'Me fixee up pipee.'

With a little thrill Hartley rose, and followed him up the length of the long room. To his delight the waiter crossed towards the curtained alcove. Holding one of these aside he ushered Hartley into a narrow passage, from which several doors opened.

'You goee in there,' he said, pointing to the first of these on the right. 'I bringee all slame pipee.'

He opened the door and Hartley found himself in a small room furnished with a low couch and a brass-topped coffee table. There was no window and the air felt curiously heavy. For a moment he sniffed that air. There was a sweetness about it that he could not place. It was not opium, and anyway, Ho-Ling would never be so foolish as to allow the drug to be smoked in a place that was so open to inspection. And then, as the pervading odour seemed to grow stronger every moment Hartley walked swiftly towards the closed door. Here he made a startling discovery. There was no handle, and moreover it fitted so closely that the blade of the penknife that he took from his pocket could hardly be forced into the space between its edge and the frame-work.

A frown gathered on his forehead, and then suddenly he heard a sound. From somewhere came a curious hissing noise.

The air of the room now was growing steadily denser. He listened for a moment intently, and then plunged a little unsteadily across the floor to the couch.

He was uncomfortably conscious of an enormous acceleration of the beating of his heart, the blood was pounding in his brain. As he caught hold of the couch to pull it aside he had to pause for a moment to loosen the constriction of his shirt band. He was suffocating! Some form of gas of an anaesthetic quality was being loosed into the room!

Too late he realized that he had been trapped. He had been put in the room to be made insensible — probably to be done to death. Obviously Li-Sin had seen through his disguise, probably someone had followed him from Harley Street. Feeling that his senses were slipping from him he put out all his strength and jerked the couch from its position against the wall. The hissing was louder now.

With eyesight failing, and with a feeling that his brain was bursting, Hartley pulled himself together sufficiently to trace instantly the source of that hissing sound. It came from the mouth of a pipe that protruded almost on the level of the floor from the wainscoting. A faint, violet vapour was pouring from it, spreading slowly like a fog over the carpet, and sending up those fumes, which were choking him and robbing him of his senses. Holding his breath he snatched his handkerchief from his pocket and stooping crammed it into the mouth of the pipe. The effort was almost too much for him. He found himself sinking to the floor. That miasmic sea of vapour engulfed his face and head; if he lay there he would be dead!

By sheer force of will he drove the machinery of his body into action. Still holding his breath he lifted his head above the cloud of vapour and by using his hands managed to rise to his feet, clutching at the edge of the couch. For some seconds he stood there, refraining with difficulty from respiration. When at last he could no longer hold his breath and he drew the scented air into his lungs he was conscious that the action of his heart increased. The physical sensation that accompanied it was not so painful. The gas, stopped at its source, was losing its effect, but still there was enough there, more than enough; to rob him of his senses if he fell.

It lay now across the floor, like a morning mist on the fields.

Very slowly and carefully Hartley placed one foot on the couch, steadied himself, followed it with the other, and then, with a swift toppling movement, mounted the high back, throwing himself against the wall as he did so for support. Now his head was some ten feet above the floor. He tested the air. Though still scented it was less heavy and produced hardly any effect as he drew it into his lungs, and it was growing purer every minute.

He waited a full minute by his watch, and finding that his eyes, which a moment before had been so distended that every object had been blurred, were now able to focus the dial accurately, then, with his legs trembling under him he stepped slowly back on to the floor.

His brain was functioning clearly once

more. He had been led into a trap, but by a piece of good fortune he had been able to escape from the snare. The question now was how might he turn the situation to his own advantage? He might play these Orientals at their own game. Obviously they expected to find him in a few minutes lying in that room either dead or unconscious. Was it possible to let them think their plan had succeeded?

Taking a piece of string from his pocket he stooped down and fastened one end of it to the handkerchief with which he had blocked the pipe, then pushing the couch back into its former position against the wall he flung himself down on the cushions in the pose of one who was unconscious. His right arm hung over the back of the couch, and in the fingers of that hand he gripped the string. The air was getting purer every moment. Lying there he waited motionless, an eternity seemed to elapse, and then his quick ear detected a faint squeaking sound beyond the door. There was a click, and instantly he pulled out the string and using his fingers only drew his handkerchief clear of the pipe and palmed it skilfully.

Somebody was crossing the floor. A claw-like hand closed upon his shoulder and he was turned face upwards on the couch. From under his partially closed eyelids he glimpsed the enigmatic face of Li-Sin. The man had a respirator tied about his mouth and was examining him with something of the detachment of a doctor. Suddenly he abandoned his examination and drawing himself erect, and with his arms folded in front of him, turned. Another man had followed him, a little Chinaman with a wizened face and a long pigtail.

'He will give no more trouble, Ho-Ling,' said the soft voice of Li-Sin. 'He sleeps the sleep of forgetfulness. Take him below. When he awakes I will deal with him.'

The little Chinaman made a sign and two men entered the room. Bending, they picked Hartley up between them, and carried him swiftly out.

He was taken along a corridor to a room at the farther end and laid on the floor while the two men drew back a carpet, disclosing a trapdoor. The trap-door was opened and once again he was lifted up. Ho-Ling entered, carrying a rope with a slipknot at one end. The noose was dropped over his head and pulled down under his arms, and then he was lowered into the abyss below.

Darkness closed round him and from somewhere came the sound of running water. He felt himself touch the ground and one of the Chinamen swarmed down the rope to his side. Rapidly he unfastened it and it was drawn up. The Chinaman half dragged and half carried him across a stone floor, opened another door and flung him into a cell-like room that was lit dimly by a blue light in the ceiling. It illumined with startling effect the impassive face and high cheekbones of the Chinaman, and then the face vanished and the door was closed and bolted upon him.

10

The Voice Beyond the Door

Dr. Hartley lay quite still until he had assured himself that he was alone, then he opened his eyes fully and sat up.

He was in a cellar, bare and unfurnished, and dimly lighted by a tinted electric globe that was screwed into the roof. Getting up he went over to the door and discovered that it was made of iron, with a lock that was unassailable even if he had any tools with which to attack it.

He had taken the precaution before leaving Harley Street, to strap under his left armpit a holster containing an automatic pistol, and this he still retained, an inexcusable act of carelessness of Li-Sin and his associates, but lucky for him. It might prove to be decidedly useful.

He was annoyed at the easy way he had been duped. No doubt he had been followed from the time he left Mallory Hall. Well, it was no use bothering about that now, the thing to do was to set about getting out of the mess he had got into, and that wasn't going to be so easy. He examined the cellar carefully. So far as he could see there was no outlet except by the door, and that was impossible, unless —

An idea suddenly came to him. If Li-Sin came to visit him or sent anyone, there was just a chance that he would be able to effect an escape.

He sat down and waited patiently, and just as he was beginning to think that nobody would come near him he heard from somewhere outside the slither of feet on the stone floor. Somebody was coming. This was the chance he had been waiting for. Noiselessly he flitted across to the door and pressed himself against the wall behind it, and there he waited, every nerve on the alert. The footsteps drew nearer. There was the sound of a key grating in the lock and the door opened. Hartley held his breath.

Ho-Ling, his black pigtail hanging

behind his back, slid across the threshold. He had hardly taken a step into the cellar when the muzzle of the doctor's automatic was pressed against his ribs.

'Put up your hands, and not a sound!' Hartley whispered. 'Go on, right up to the ceiling.'

The man's hands went over his head, With a swift movement Hartley examined his captive's clothing, removing a long, wicked knife which he carried concealed in his breast.

'Get over into the centre of the room,' he went on. 'And hurry!'

The Chinaman did so, his almond eyes watching the doctor closely.

'Take off your belt and give it to me,' said Hartley.

The man did as he was told. Hartley drew closer to him, dropping the belt on the floor.

'Look up at that light,' he commanded softly.

The Chinaman raised his eyes to the blue-tinted globe and as he did so Hartley brought up his clenched fist with all his force to the man's jaw. It made contact neatly and accurately with the point, and the Chinaman shot backwards and collapsed on the floor.

'That anaesthetic will only last for a few minutes, anyway,' muttered Hartley, 'but it's long enough for me.'

Putting his automatic into his pocket he picked up the belt. A few seconds later, with the aid of his handkerchief and a section of his coat lining he had bound and gagged Ho-Ling effectively. Then he went to the open door. Closing it behind him he locked it and put the key into his pocket. Then he looked about him. All was darkness, but he had matches in his pocket and striking one of these he looked about.

So far as he could tell he appeared to be in a cellar larger than the one he had just left. He could still hear the sound of running water and stooping down he discovered that it came from the floor beneath his feet.

'Some disused drain flowing into the Thames, I suppose,' he muttered to himself.

Examining the ceiling he saw the

trapdoor from which he had been lowered, but it appeared to be all of eighteen feet above his head and there was no ladder available by which he could reach it. For a moment it seemed to him that he was as much a prisoner in that vault as he had been in the cellar from which he had just escaped. But there must be some means of exit, and that exit he must find. He struck another match and walked down the centre of the vault, with the sound of running water still in his ears. On either side of him was an abyss of darkness, which the feeble flame of the match failed to penetrate. He reached the end of the cellar to find himself faced by a high brick wall and an iron door, similar to the one leading to the cellar from which he had just escaped. He tried the handle; it was locked. He was turning away when a faint sob reached him, muffled, like that of someone in pain.

'Jack!' wailed a voice. 'Oh, Jack!'

Hartley's jaw dropped, and over his face came an expression of absolute amazement. The voice that came from behind the door was the voice of Jill Mallory!

Recovering from his astonishment he stooped down and put his ear to the keyhole. The sobbing had started again, he could hear it more distinctly now, and mingled with it occasionally was a little moan of pain. How had Jill got to the Oriental den? How had she been caught in the net that Li-Sin had spread?

He struck a third match and examined the door. The lock was similar to that of the other one, and he had no instrument with which he could hope to open it, but he must get the girl out somehow. A moment's consideration satisfied him that there was no use in going back to the cellar he himself had occupied and searching again the prisoner he had left there. If that man was the general gaoler he hadn't the keys of the two cells in his possession. He had satisfied himself on that point when he had examined the man's clothing for any concealed weapons. Probably the keys were left above and only the one immediately required brought by the man on his visit to this underground dungeon.

Suddenly another alternative occurred to him. There might be only one key, a master key, which would open both the doors, the key which was in his pocket! He pulled it out and fitted it into the lock. To his immense relief he felt the bolt give as he turned it, another moment and he had swung the door back and stepped across the threshold.

There was silence now. The sobs and moans of pain had ceased. It almost seemed to him as if the girl in the cell, unseen as yet, was holding her breath. Again he struck a match, and saw that this cellar was in a worse condition than the one in which he had been put. The floor was reeking with damp and the stone walls were running with water. Clusters of cobwebs dangled from the ceiling and then he saw Jill.

The girl was standing bolt upright against the opposite wall staring at him, and a little shudder of horror and loathing passed over Hartley, as he saw the reason for her unnatural position. She was held in an upright position by ropes, which had been secured with staples driven into the stone work. A strand of rope stretched horizontally kept her neck tightly against the wall, but the devilishness of the treatment to which she was being subjected did not end there. From a small tin cistern fixed on the roof a little spray of water played continually upon her bonds. He realized instantly the meaning of this device. The water would contract the hemp, and the ropes would tighten until, after an eternity of pain, the victim would lose consciousness. Even as this realization flashed across his mind the girl's voice broke the stillness. It was hot with anger.

'What have you done to him, you brute?' she demanded. 'Where is he?'

And then Hartley realized that his own face was invisible in the gloom. She had mistaken him for the Chinese gaoler!

11

Prisoners of Li-Sin

'Hush, Jill,' he called quietly, 'don't make a sound.'

He heard her little cry of astonishment and, taking the knife which he had found on the Chinaman, he groped a way across the cellar.

'Steady,' he whispered reassuringly. 'Steady. My poor child, don't struggle or you'll hurt yourself.'

He struck another one of his matches, and then with swift movements of his knife he severed the ropes that held her, and caught her in his arms as she fainted. The sudden shock of his appearance, coming on the top of her ordeal had proved too much for her. Hartley thought swiftly. At the present moment the girl was in no condition to attempt to escape from that underground dungeon. Until she had recovered consciousness he could do nothing. Laying her gently on the floor he chafed her raw wrists, and soaking his handkerchief in the water that still dripped from the cistern he bathed her face. After a little while her eyelids fluttered, and presently she was staring up at him in utter bewilderment.

'Dr. Hartley,' she stammered, in a voice which showed she hardly credited her senses.

Hartley laid his hand gently on her shoulder.

'Don't talk just yet,' he said. 'You'll want all your strength presently.'

With his last match he examined the cellar and presently found outside the door embedded in the wall, a light switch. Pressing it he flooded the place with the same bluish light as the other cellar.

'Now,' he said, 'quickly, how did you get here?'

'You 'phoned for both of us to come,' she replied.

'I?' he echoed. 'I didn't 'phone at all.'

'No, I realize that now,' she replied. 'It was a trick, and it succeeded. They've got Jack as well!'

Briefly she told him what had happened. A telephone call had come through to Mallory Hall and Jack had recognized his voice. He had asked them to come to Ho-Ling's and when they had arrived they had been met by Ho-Ling himself, who had taken them through the restaurant and into a small room where he had asked them to wait. While there they had been overcome by the same gas as had been used in the case of Dr. Hartley.

'Where is Jack?' asked Hartley.

The girl shook her head.

'I don't know,' she answered. 'When I recovered consciousness I found myself as you found me.'

He heard a sound from the larger cellar, and peering out quickly was just in time to see the trap in the roof opening. Swiftly he made up his mind.

'Get back against the wall,' he whispered softly, 'and stand as you were standing before. Leave the rest to me.'

Hurrying to the door he locked it on the outside and crouched against the wall in the darkness. A square of light had appeared on the floor of the larger room from the trapdoor above, and even as he looked a man began to descend by means of a rope. As his feet touched the floor Hartley was seized by a spasm of frantic anxiety. Supposing he went to the cell that he himself had occupied he might be able to give the alarm before he could be stopped. It was with a feeling of real relief that he saw the Chinaman with his typical Oriental slouch coming towards the door near which he crouched.

Nerving himself as the man fitted the key in the lock the doctor stepped noiselessly forward and brought the butt of his pistol down, just behind the other's ear. He dropped to the floor like a stone and lay still. Bending over him Hartley made a rapid examination of his clothing, then opening the cellar door he called to Jill:

'Give me some of those ropes,' he said. 'We'll tie this brute up so that he can't do any more harm.'

Having fastened the man's ankles and wrists he completed the business by tying him to one of the rings in the wall

'You wait here, Jill,' he whispered, 'while I go and examine the trapdoor. There's more than a possibility there may be someone waiting about.'

What he was to do in such an eventuality he was completely at a loss for the moment to think. He would be reduced once more to the problem that he himself had had to consider, of finding an exit by the tunnel, which carried the running water he could hear flowing below the floor of the cellar. But no one was visible when he peered cautiously up through the gap in the floor above. The rope was dangling as the Chinaman had left it. He beckoned swiftly to the girl.

'I'm going to climb up,' he whispered. 'When I'm at the top make a loop and slip it under your arm, then hold on to the rope and I'll pull you up.'

Hand over hand he swarmed up. When he reached the floor above he took a swift glance round. The room in which the trap opened, the door had been left ajar, evidently to facilitate the return of the Chinaman, and the first thing he did was to close it. Then moving back quickly to the edge of the trapdoor he pulled Jill up. It required all his strength and he was immensely relieved when the girl, clutching at the end of the trap, scrambled to safety.

'Jack's somewhere in this house,' she said in a whisper. 'We can't go without him.'

He nodded and crossing to the door he opened it noiselessly and slipped out into the passage beyond. He could hear a murmur of voices coming from a room on his immediate left. Stooping down by the door he listened. The unmistakable voice of Li-Sin speaking in Chinese came to his ears. He applied his eye to the keyhole.

He had a vision of the interior, furnished with all the sumptuousness of the East. The walls were hung with draperies on which sprawled great green dragons. Seated in a low chair with his back towards him was the figure of Li-Sin, and immediately in front of him was what looked like a surgical table. On this was stretched the figure of Jack Mallory, with his wrists bound to the top and his ankles similarly tied to the bottom!

Even as he looked a Chinaman came into view, bowing low before the seated figure of Li-Sin and handing him something that gleamed brightly in the light. Hartley felt his blood run cold as he saw that it was a surgical knife. Li-Sin rose slowly to his feet and approaching the prone figure of Mallory bent over his bared back.

Hartley acted quickly. Pulling out his revolver he grasped the handle of the door and twisting it, flung it open.

'Put up your hands, Li-Sin,' he said sternly.

The tall Chinaman straightened up, and if he was surprised to see Hartley no sign of it appeared on his impassive face. He gave an almost imperceptible shrug and at the same instant stepped quickly backwards. Before Hartley realized what was happening he had reached the wall. There was a click and the man had disappeared. The little Chinaman sprang at him, and hastily clubbing the weapon Hartley brought it down on his head. He knew that there was a secret panel in the wall at the spot where Li-Sin had disappeared but he had no time to examine it. He had two persons' lives in his hands, Jack Mallory and Jill. He must get them out of this den before the house was roused. Li-Sin had escaped and it was clear that his first act would be to take steps to prevent his prisoners from slipping through his fingers.

Hartley sprang back towards the bed and with the knife that he had carried in his pocket cut the ropes that bound Jack.

'Quick,' he exclaimed. 'Follow me. We haven't a moment to lose!'

The young man scrambled off the operating table and together they rushed out of the room into the corridor. In another moment he was at Jill's side.

'Come on,' he exclaimed. 'We must find a way to the street. 'I've got him.'

A little cry of joy came from the girl's lips as the white-faced dishevelled figure of her husband came into the room.

'Come on,' said Hartley. 'We've got to find the front door somehow.'

As he uttered the word he dashed back

into the hall. Even as he did so there reached the deep notes of a gong. Its reverberating sound grew louder and louder and then as it rose to a deeper boom there was mingled with it a noise like the rustling of rats behind a wainscoting. With a feeling of despair Hartley slipped back across the threshold. To go any farther might be fatal. He had no idea which direction to take and while he was seeking about his unseen foes might be upon him.

He came to a sudden decision. There was still a way of retreat — if not into the free air of the street at least to a place where he could hold for sometime. There was the vault where he had been taken prisoner. As he came to that decision he turned quickly, his arms stretched out.

'Go back,' he exclaimed, shepherding his two companions into the room again, 'and down through the trapdoor, both of you. Hurry!'

Closing the door he locked it, and taking his position up turned to watch the movements of the others. The girl had already disappeared down the rope, he saw Jack launch himself into space.

As he too vanished there was a crashing blow on the door and through the splintered framework appeared the steel head of an axe.

Hartley sprang for the opening in the floor but even at this moment of crisis his brain functioned rapidly. He must not only think about his immediate escape, he must consider the future when they would have to stand siege in the room below. Although the door was already being reduced to matchwood he coolly lifted the flap of the trapdoor and keeping it open with his body felt for and found the rope. As he let himself slide down it the door closed with a muffled bang behind him. The next moment he was in the cellar below. Above him he could hear racing feet, a ray of light filtered through from the darkened roof above. It widened and widened as the trapdoor was pulled back.

Hartley looking up, pistol in hand, waited till that widening space showed the figures of two men, then he pressed the trigger. As the sound of the explosion went echoing deafeningly through the vault the trapdoor closed with a bang and a profound darkness settled down.

Above he could hear the faint patter of feet, then these restless movements ceased and the silence of the grave fell. For a time, at any rate, he and his two companions were safe. Whispers reached him from the gloom, whispers and what sounded like a kiss. A smile curled his lips for a moment. No need to disturb them he reflected as he kept his back towards the spot from which the sound came, but he must think of the future.

They were safe for a little while, but how long would their immunity last?

He tried to deal with all the possibilities of the situation. There were just two courses, as far as he could see, open to the enemy above. They must either try a surprise attack through the trapdoor or they must wait till their victims were compelled to surrender by hunger. Against the first possibility he could take an easy precaution. The rope by which they descended was still in position. The trapdoor could not be opened without the rope being moved. Taking the heavy key which he no longer needed from his pocket, he fastened it to the end of the rope in such a way that any vibration of the line must make the metal clink against the stone pavement, and so warn them of what was afoot.

But how they were going to defend themselves against the effects of a long siege was a more difficult matter. They were without food. There was water, however, he remembered that could be drawn from the cistern in the cellar in which Jill had been confined, unless, of course, the Chinese gang cut off the supply, but he had to face the facts that they could be starved into surrender unless they could find a means of escape from that cellar. That indeed was their only chance. Having made up his mind on that point Hartley swept all other considerations aside and devoted his thoughts to the problem.

Lying down full length he put his ear to the ground. The murmur of that running water which he had heard since he had first been brought into the cellar became louder and more distinct. It was obvious that below the paving there was a conduit of some kind, a tunnel that must have an exit as the water was flowing. But how to get to that tunnel? They had no tools; with their bare hands it would be impossible to shift those massive blocks of stone and lay bare the opening beneath. Perhaps there was something in the cellar itself that would help them.

'Come here, Jack,' he called.

Mallory came towards him out of the gloom.

'Take this pistol, and if anybody opens the trapdoor, fire.'

With the doors of the two end cellars opened sufficient light filtered into the larger vault for him to see, and he began a search that ended, at first in disappointment, and then he found something which raised his hopes. Almost completely hidden between the bricks in one of the walls he came upon a little rusty projection that was not a nail and was not a staple, but something that looked like a tiny lever. Grasping it Hartley pulled it down with all his might. It refused to

116

budge. He pushed it up and this time it moved. At the same instant, from the floor beneath his feet came a faint rumbling sound, and looking down saw one of the slabs begin to move!

The roar of the water below grew louder and louder as the stone continued to revolve until its upper part was at right angles to the floor.

Dropping on his knees Hartley leaned over the edge and peered into the opening. He could see nothing at first, but after a little while his eyes got accustomed to the gloom and he saw a tunnel, over six feet high, in which a rush of water was flowing. From far away it seemed there reached his ears a louder splashing, as if the water fell over some kind of weir. He concluded that eventually it must reach the river, and if there was no grating the tunnel offered a chance of escape.

He called to the others and showed them what he had found.

'I'll go first,' he said. 'Jill can follow and hold on to my waist, and you, Jack, bring up the rear.'

Swinging his legs over the edge of the tunnel he dropped into the water below. It ran, he noticed, almost up to his knees. Moving forward a little he waited until the girl had taken up her position behind him, and a final splash told him that Jack had also joined the party.

'Hold tight!' he exclaimed, and waded off into the darkness ahead of him.

The air was foul and the water was very cold, and twice they were delayed by Jill losing her footing. Hartley's anxiety increased every moment, for in that pitch darkness he could see nothing, neither could he hear, for the roar of the water was like thunder in their ears. And then, abruptly it seemed, the speed of the flowing water in which they were wading decreased. Not only was it growing more sluggish, but it was rising at every step they took, and now it was up to their waists, Hartley was pushing forward neck high. Instantly it dawned upon him what was happening! They were approaching the exit to the tunnel where the stream they were following flowed in to the Thames. The tide of the river was rising, they had not a moment to lose, In another moment they would be forced to retreat, already the surface of the water was touching his chin, and then, at that moment, a red light flashed across his vision. It was the light of a tug. They were close to the exit, but in that race against the tide, they would hardly have a minute to spare.

'Hold tight, both of you,' he gasped. 'We're just there.'

As he spoke, and as he felt the girl's clasp tighten round his waist, he plunged forward. The next instant he was almost swept off his feet, which had sunk deep in the mud of the river's bed. Then the breath of the night was on his face and he could see the stars shining in the sky.

'Steady,' he whispered. 'Don't leave go or you may be swept away.'

The tunnel from which they had escaped ran out under a wharf, and its mouth from which they had emerged was almost completely covered by the lap of the rising tide. They had only just done it, and they were very far from being safe yet. They would have to swim until they could find a landing place, and then, ten yards away from them, up the river, Hartley saw that a boat was moored.

As soon as his eyes lighted upon it he decided on his course of action. This was the swiftest and surest way of escape. Once aboard that boat they could row to the comparative safety of the opposite bank.

He explained to Jack and Jill his intention.

'I'm going to swim to that boat and bring it back,' he said. 'You two hang on here to these piles and wait for me.'

He struck out for the boat and in a few seconds he had been swept against its mooring rope. Gripping this he felt his way along to the bows and raising himself got his legs over the side. There were oars in the bottom, he saw to his relief, and jerking these into the rowlocks took out his knife and cut the mooring ropes, then, swinging himself into the seat he began to row back towards the two figures of his companions.

As he came along side them Jill uttered a little cry.

'Look,' she said.

Hartley looked round, and as he did so, from the bank came a yell. He saw a number of Chinamen gesticulating wildly and scuttling down the steps of the wharf to a boat that lay moored there. So Li-Sin had discovered their escape and was after them? There was not a moment to lose. He hauled Jack and the girl into the boat and bent to the oars, sending it sweeping away from the bank against the tide.

His pursuers were fifty yards in his wake, he was just settling down to a vigorous stroke when there was an ominous crack and one of the oars broke in his hand. Hartley seldom wasted time in swearing but at the moment he came very near to it. They were helpless now, already caught by the tide the boat was swinging up stream. From behind he could hear an excited chattering. His pursuers were drawing ever nearer. He could see their faces in the gloom, and he knew what fate awaited them if they were caught!

At that moment a tug, towing behind it a string of barges, swept down upon them. Picking up the only sound oar Hartley rushed to the stern and began to propel the boat out of harm's way. The tug swept by them, missing them by inches, with the captain on the bridge cursing them roundly. Hartley looked back. The pursuing boat, as though fearful of attracting the attention of the tugs was just maintaining its position on the tide, the rowers merely paddling. Once, however, the tug had passed out of view, the gang, he realized, would resume their pursuit. Suddenly he had an inspiration.

'Stand by to make fast, Jack,' he shouted. 'Grab anything you can get hold of!'

Working his oar frantically he drove the boat against the line of barges, as she bumped against the second of the string and nearly capsized Jack made a grab at the rope hanging from the barge and missed. A moment later and the third barge was swinging past them, Again Hartley drove the boat towards the tug's tow, and again Jack missed. Only one barge remained now, the last. As if realizing what depended upon him Mallory braced himself in the bows and fixed his eyes on the barge.

'Now!' he exclaimed.

In answer to that cry Hartley gave the boat just that necessary amount of impetus. Flinging himself forward Jack grabbed and held on to a stout, round, hemp fender, that hung over the side of the barge. He was almost dragged from the boat to which he clung with his feet.

'Quick!' he shouted. 'Quick! I can't hold on much longer!'

Dropping the oar Hartley staggered forward. Seizing a rope that was coiled up in the stern he balanced himself perilously for a second on the gunwale of the little vessel and then, catching hold of the fender as well, managed to make the line fast. The next moment they were driving forward down the river in the wake of the string of barges.

For the space of nearly a minute the three fugitives sat motionless, staring at one another. They had escaped! Looking back they could see that the gang had abandoned their pursuit, Jill was the first to break the silence.

'I'm terribly cold,' she said, shivering.

'So am I,' said Jack through his chattering teeth. 'But I don't think it will be long now before we can get warm. Anyway, we're out of that Hellhole, which is something to be thankful for!'

Two hours later they were sitting before a roaring fire in Harley Street, and relating to an interested Eric their thrilling adventures of the night.

12

Li-Sin Strikes Again

Three days went by without any signs that Li-Sin was on earth. On Hartley's advice Jack and Jill had moved from Mallory Hall, and come back to their flat in town. Except for one room, the decorators had completed their job, and they were able to do this without very much discomfort. Hartley concluded that London would be safer for them than the country, and to a large extent he was right, though events were to prove that even in the heart of the West End the hand of Li-Sin could make itself felt.

The doctor had rung up Gladwin early on the morning following their escape from Ho-Ling's and the inspector had organised a raid, with the assistance of K division, but the raiders had found nothing. When they reached the premises they were deserted.

Ho-Ling had disappeared and with him every one in the building. Not even the Chinese waiter was left. They made several interesting discoveries, however, one of which was, that the Chinaman had evidently run an organised opium den and gambling house. The vault from which Hartley and the others had escaped was only one of three that stretched underneath the building, and the other two were fitted up luxuriantly, with silken hangings and cushioned divans. Of Li-Sin there was no sign, and it seemed, after an examination of the building, that he had never lived there. Probably he had only used the place to meet the rest of his gang, and had another hideout where he lived,

'We've got to find him,' said Dr. Hartley, sitting in Inspector Gladwin's office at Scotland Yard one afternoon. 'None of us are safe until he's been captured.'

'That's easier said than done,' said the inspector gloomily. 'He may be any-where.'

'Personally,' answered the doctor, 'I

don't think he's very far away. You can take it from me that these two setbacks he's had are not going to alter his determination to revenge himself on myself and the Mallorys. This period of quiet is merely the calm before the storm, a breathing space during which he can mature his plans.'

'Well, when he makes a move we may be able to get him,' said the inspector. 'Until he shows his hand I'm afraid we can do nothing. The police are on the look out for him, I've warned every section in the country, but as long as he lies low he's pretty safe. You know, Doctor,' he looked across at the man opposite him, 'this fellow can't be Li-Sin. I've been thinking it over since I last saw you. The Chinese may be clever, but they can't piece together a man who was blown into a thousand fragments.'

'I agree with you,' said Hartley. 'And in my opinion I think you're right.'

'To Western eyes, one Chinaman,' went on Gladwin, 'is very much like another. It wouldn't be difficult for a man to pass himself off as Li-Sin, and those marks on his chest which he showed you could quite easily be faked, though why he should take the trouble, I'm hanged if I know.'

'It's just the sort of thing that would appeal to a Chinaman,' said Hartley. 'And at the back of it, you must remember, is a certain amount of superstition. No doubt this man who says he's Li-Sin firmly believes it himself. He is probably under the impression that the soul of Li-Sin has temporarily taken up its possession in his body in order to carry out this feud of vengeance.'

'Sounds stupid to me,' grunted Gladwin.

'It may do,' answered Hartley. 'But the Chinese mentality is different from yours.'

They chatted for some time and then Hartley took his leave. He had arranged to lunch with Jack Mallory at his club and arrived a little late, to find the young man already waiting for him.

'Well, Jack, how are things?' he asked, 'Any more trouble?'

Mallory shook his head.

'No.' he replied. 'I'm glad to say we've neither heard nor seen anything of our friend. Perhaps he's given it up.'

Hartley shook his head.

'Don't you believe it,' he said. 'This quietness only means that he is preparing something. He may even want to let us think he is giving it up so as to put us off our guard. Don't you allow yourself to be lulled into a false sense of security.'

They had an excellent lunch. Jill, it appeared, was spending the afternoon at one of the big stores shopping, and Jack was calling for her at seven at a friend's house, where she was going to tea. They had arranged to go to the theatre in the evening, and that would just give them time to go home and dress.

They sat for some time in the smoking room after lunch, chatting about various things, but although the conversation ranged from books to bridge at the back of their minds they had only one interest; the menace of the sinister Chinaman who was lurking somewhere in the shadows, waiting to spring.

Jack had tea with Hartley and afterwards they played a game of billiards. At a quarter to seven Mallory left, driving away in a taxi. Hartley went back to the smoking room and ordered a glass of sherry. He was dining at Home but it was too early yet to leave the club. Picking up an evening paper he read it, sipping his drink. He was half dozing in front of the big fire when a page came in and informed him that he was wanted on the telephone.

He went out to the little cubicles that housed the telephones. Picking up the receiver he applied it to his ear, and Jack's voice, sharp with anxiety, reached him.

'Hello? Is that Hartley? Listen, Jill never turned up for tea!'

'Where are you 'phoning from?' asked the doctor quickly.

'Mrs. Manson's,' answered Jack, 'where Jill was supposed to have tea. I'm terribly worried — '

'I'll come and see you,' said Hartley. 'Where can I find you?'

'Harford Mansions, Piccadilly.' answered Mallory.

Hartley rang off, and stopping only to get his hat and coat from the cloakroom left the club and hailed a taxi.

In the big block of flats where Mrs. Manson lived he found Jack Mallory waiting anxiously, and with him a pretty fair-haired woman, who looked equally worried.

'I can't understand it,' she said. 'Jill is usually so punctual. She promised she'd be here not later than five.'

'Perhaps she was later at the store than she expected,' said Hartley, 'and has gone straight home. Have you 'phoned the flat?'

Jack shook his head.

'No, I'll do that now,' he said, but when he came back there was no lightening of his worried expression. 'She's not there,' he said.

'Is it likely she'd be still at the store?' suggested Hartley.

'She would have 'phoned, surely,' said Mrs. Manson. 'Jill is always so particular about that sort of thing. If she breaks an appointment she always lets you know.'

'I suppose they know her fairly well at

the store?' said Hartley, addressing Jack.

Mallory nodded.

'Oh, yes, they know her quite well.'

'Then let's go along there,' said the doctor.

They drove to the stores and interviewed the commissionaire. He knew Mrs. Mallory well; she had been there practically the whole afternoon and had left about half-past four. He had himself called her a taxi and escorted her to it.

'Where did she tell the driver to go to?' asked Hartley.

'Harford Mansions, sir,' answered the commissionaire, and Jack's heart sank.

'Is it possible she could have met with an accident?' he muttered, but Dr. Hartley shook his head.

'If she had you'd have heard of it by now,' he answered. 'No, I'm afraid there's only one explanation, that damned fiend's got her!' And Jack groaned.

13

What Happened to Jill

Jill spent a pleasant afternoon buying and ordering a number of things for her newly-decorated flat. The time passed so quickly that four o'clock came almost before she realized it. She hurried the rest of her purchases, arranged for the majority of them to be sent and made her way to the entrance of the store. The commissionaire touched his hat as he recognized her and she asked him to get her a taxi. There was one crawling along by the pavement and he hailed it. The cab came to a halt, and crossing the pavement he held open the door while she got in.

'Where to, Madam?' he asked.

'Harford Mansions, Piccadilly,' she said.

He repeated this to the driver, accepted the generous tip which Jill thrust into his hand with a smile, closed the door and as the taxi drove off returned to his post.

Jill leaned back on the cushioned seat and opening her bag took out her little flat cigarette case and helped herself to a cigarette. She was pleasantly tired and looking forward to the tea that awaited her at the end of her journey. She decided that she would cut her visit short to Mrs. Manson, and go home early so that she could have a short rest before it was time to dress to accompany Jack to the show they had planned. Yes, she felt extraordinarily tired and the air of the taxi was unusually close. She crushed out her half-smoked cigarette in the ashtray and leaned forward to open the window, but it stuck and she couldn't shift it. A peculiar heavy feeling was creeping over her and she found a difficulty in breathing. There was a strange, sweetish smell in the air, which at first she had put down to the perfume used by a previous fare. It was momentarily growing stronger and she found that she was breathing quickly and irregularly and she leaned forward to tap on the window to attract the attention of the driver and as she did so everything went black . . .

How long she remained unconscious she never knew but she recovered her sense slowly to the accompaniment of a racking misery that was crawling to life in her nerves. Her head throbbed maddeningly and every heartbeat seemed to be bumping its way through her temples against a vast compression. She was in a bath of perspiration, and there was a feverish heat in her flesh that seemed to be consuming her. She tried to sit up but the effort was beyond her, there was a palsy in her muscles, a flabbiness that rendered them lifeless.

She tried to collect her thoughts but her mind refused to concentrate. She was no longer in the cab but in a room with a light. She closed her eyes and relaxed, the streaming light a few feet above her head tendered them and hurt, cutting into her head like knives and giving her a feeling of sickness. She felt for the moment as though she was being rapidly revolved in a spinning drum with no chance of either stopping it or getting out. For many minutes she lay back slipping back again into a state of comatose lethargy.

Full consciousness began to return to her in a series of growing waves, each recurring wave seeming to leave in its wake a greater and more profound sea of depression.

It was half-an-hour before she had strength to move her body and the action brought with it violent physical pain. She did not want to move, did not want to think, did not even want to breathe; it would have been a blessed relief to have quietly sunk away into oblivion, to have closed her eyes and let death have its way with her. She did not want to live; an ocean of melancholic depression encompassed her.

Gradually she opened her eyes again. The blinding light came from a lamp in the big ceiling above her and looking round she saw that she was in a narrow room, along one side of which was a row of round windows. There was a gentle undulating motion and with a gasp of surprise she realized that she was on a boat of some description. She was lying in a bunk and as memory came flooding back she realized what had happened. Vaguely she pieced together the fleeting fragments that her memory cast up. She had got into that taxi and in some way had been drugged. It occurred to her to look at the time by her wristwatch. The hands pointed to half-past-two, but whether this was in the morning or afternoon she had no idea. Certainly no light came in through the portholes, but then it was quite possible that they were obscured by shutters.

Her eyes wandered vaguely round the room. It was about ten feet square and the bunk in which she was lying was strewn with silken cushions. The walls were covered with beautifully worked tapestries. At the far end a gross figure of an enormous Buddha, solid and complacent, gazed inscrutably down upon her. It was a hugely magnified counterpart of the one in jade, which adorned the mantel-piece in her own flat. The squat bulk of it sat ponderously on a black ebony pedestal and its eyes were focussed on a small, oblong crate at its feet. A rich, heavily piled carpet covered the floor.

With a violent effort of will she sat up, her head swam dizzily, every nerve seemed to be quivering in fierce protest. She put up her hand to her bosom and feeling something under her fingers looked down, and saw a note pinned there.

The message on it had been printed in pencil:

'Should you require anything there is a bell-push in the bulkhead to your right.'

There was no signature but the formation of the pencilled letters told her who had written it. Li-Sin!

She crumpled the note into a ball and shuddered. Her mind, weakened by the drug that had been administered to her was incapable of grappling with the situation. She felt a wild panic stealing through her. In a startled effort to find a way of escape she swayed to her feet. For a moment she stood reeling and then almost fell, and would have fallen except that she clutched the edge of the bunk to save herself. Her knees had no strength in them. She hauled herself back and sank down among the cushions and wondered what fate the Chinaman had in store for her.

It was almost impossible that she could escape this time, impossible that either Jack or Hartley could ever find her, she didn't even know where she was herself. She lay back and forced herself to be calm, and gradually she succeeded. Her head was getting clearer and the physical sickness was wearing off. Presently she got up and walked weakly round the apartment, and curiously enough the first thing she looked for was a mirror, but Li-Sin's prison had not been arranged to accommodate the requirements of a lady. The walls, rich in the luxury of priceless tapestries, were destitute of mirrors.

She inspected the great Buddha. It was carved out of a curiously smooth oily stone, like soap stone, but of a far finer texture, with much more beautiful graining. It was huge, towering up to the ceiling, and as firmly planted as a statue.

The whole place was overpoweringly hot, without a single means of ventilation so far as she could see, and the cabin had acquired a stuffiness that made and kept her drowsy. As she had suspected, outside the portholes shutters had been screwed. Dimly she heard the wail of a tugboat's siren, and the rocking motion increased as the boat passed. That meant that she was somewhere on the river, but what part of the river she had no idea.

She continued to wander round the room. On the floor near the bunk she saw her shoes, which somebody had taken off, and put them on. With them was her handbag, she picked it up and opening it, produced a tiny mirror let into the flap. When she had powdered her face and tidied her hair she felt better. There was a table in the centre of the place and for the first time she became aware that it contained a tray covered by a serviette. She lifted this and found quite a palatable meal. There were some slices of breast of chicken, a plate of bread fingers, a little silver bowl of fruit and a glass of Burgundy and some water. The last thing in the world she felt like doing was eating, but apparently Li-Sin had no intention of starving her, probably he had planned something infinitely more dreadful. She went back to the bunk and lying down tried to think things out, but so far as she could see there was no way out, she would just have to lie there and make the best of it. Suddenly she realized that that was the very worst thing she could do. Although it seemed hopeless it was no good giving in without a struggle. She got up again and walked about. She found that she felt better walking about.

It occurred to her that in her previous examination of the room, she had seen no door, and she began to look for one. She knew there must be one somewhere, or a trapdoor in the floor. She hunted round, searching behind the silken hangings, and she found nothing. With difficulty she rolled back the great carpet and underneath was nothing but the deck planking; thick, heavy, and as solidly founded as the day the ship came off the slip.

She sat down again and reaching for her bag found and lit a cigarette. She discovered that there were seven left in her case, and uttered a prayer of thankfulness. They would help to soothe her jumping nerves, anyway. While she smoked, for some reason she could not define, her attention was attracted again to the great Buddha.

Sitting on the bunk she stared at it, and then the possibility occurred to her that there might be some secret opening controlled from some fitment attached to the great God. She got up again and crossed over, peering behind the image, but it was flat against the far wall and much too bulky to have been shifted. She inspected it from every angle and there did not seem to be anything suspicious anywhere in its massive frame. She pushed and pulled and tugged but every inch of the idol was as solid as Gibraltar. And then she pressed the plate that rested at the feet and felt the whole thing depress itself half an inch. There was a soft click and the carved robe of the god opened out like a door.

The inside of it was hollow; she peered into the cavity. It was like a cupboard and on the shelf was a small silver case, beautifully chased and lined with puffed silk, but it was the contents that sent a sparkle to her eyes, for it contained a little crystal bottle and a silver hypodermic syringe. She hurriedly took out the bottle, uncorked it and poured the contents on the floor, under one corner of the carpet. Carefully washing it out she refilled it with some water from the jug on one table and put it back where she had found it. If the drug was intended to be used on her it was now harmless.

She had just closed the cupboard when she heard a sound that seemed to come from somewhere near her. Tiptoeing back to the bunk she kicked off her shoes and lying down began to breathe in long, steady exhalations. The sound came again and now she located it. It was immediately on the right of the giant idol. It was vague, like the scratching of mice, and through half closed eyes she watched. Slowly the tall panel revolved on a central pivot until it was swung out squarely into the room. Through the oblong opening a tall figure entered, it came slowly into the room and gently closed the panel behind it. It was Li-Sin.

He was dressed in his ceremonial robes of rich blue silk, embroidered with a riot of marvellous colouring. He raised his arms and bowed to the Buddha, and the sleeves of his robes feel away revealing his yellow wrists and skinny forearms.

Jill lay motionless as he came towards her and he stood by the side of the bunk, his hands concealed in his loose sleeves, staring down at her. The lined yellow face was expressionless, and for nearly a minute she bore his scrutiny maintaining a quiet sane sleep as he bent over her, listening to her half inaudible respiration. Presently he exhaled a long hissing breath, and, going over to the Buddha made another profound obeisance and pressed on the tray. The cupboard opened and he took out the hypodermic case. With deft, practised fingers he took the syringe, fitted it together, inserted it in the neck of the bottle and extracted a measured dose.

Holding it up to the light he examined it. There appeared to be a little too much for his requirements for he carefully squirted a few drops back into the bottle.

There was humour in his taking such meticulous pains over a drop of pure totally innocuous water, but the comedy of it was lost on Jill. She was beginning to feel horribly nervous. He came back to the bunk and put the syringe carefully on the floor beside her, then stooping, he took her wrists and felt her pulse. Apparently he was satisfied for with his other hand he picked up the syringe. Pulling back her sleeve he pinched up a little ridge of flesh and plunged the needle into her arm. There was scarcely any pain and he pushed the plunger home. When he had done this he went back to the idol, unscrewed the syringe, put it back in its case and closed the cupboard. Turning, he looked at her again and then nodded slowly, as if satisfied. Going to the panel by which he had entered he pressed on the floor with his foot, it opened and the tall robed figure passed through. The next second she was alone and the panel was closed again.

Her heart was beating with excitement and hope, for she had noticed the exact spot on the floor where his foot had pressed and worked the secret entrance, and, although he did not know it she was as wide-awake as ever she had been in her life!

14

Suspense

Jack Mallory was in a state bordering on distraction as they left the store.

'What can we do?' he growled. 'God knows what may have happened to Jill by now and we can't do anything.'

'It's no good getting in a panic,' said Hartley soothingly. 'I know how you feel and I feel pretty much the same, but we shan't do any good unless we remain cool.'

'Cool!' exclaimed Jack, clenching his fists. 'How do you expect me to be cool when I know that Jill is in the power of that fiend?'

'I know it's difficult,' said the doctor, 'but you won't do any good by being anything else.'

It was some time before he could quiet Jack but at last he succeeded.

'Well, what are we going to do?' he

demanded. 'We must do something.'

'We're going along to the Yard,' said Hartley. 'The first thing to do is to find out if that taxi can be traced.'

He held up his hand and a cab swerved into the kerb. He pushed Jack inside and telling the driver to go to Scotland Yard, got in beside him.

Inspector Gladwin was on the point of leaving for the day when they were shown into his office.

'Hello, what's the matter?' he said at the sight of their grave faces.

Hartley explained briefly, and the inspector's heavy face grew stern.

'The man's a devil,' he grunted. 'However, we may be able to find a trace of that cab.'

He picked up a telephone at his elbow and barked an order. For some minutes he was speaking rapidly while they sat and watched him in silence, then he hung up the, receiver and wiped his face.

'That may do some good,' he said. 'I've had an 'All stations' call sent out to pull in the driver of the cab who picked up a young lady outside Harridge's Stores at

148

four-thirty this afternoon. I'll arrange for a broadcast message in the last news tonight, asking the driver of the cab to come forward, and a squad of plain clothes men are going to comb the garages and ranks.'

'Is that all you can do?' growled Jack.

'I'm afraid it is, sir,' said Gladwin sympathetically. 'If we can find the driver of the cab he'll be able to tell us where he set Mrs. Mallory down.'

'If he did!' said Hartley quietly. 'I'm rather inclined to believe that the cab and the driver were in the pay of Li-Sin.'

'In that case,' said the inspector, it's going to be a difficult job.'

'It's going to be a difficult job anyway,' broke in Jack. 'We haven't the least idea where to begin looking even.'

Privately Gladwin thought that it was an impossible job, but he kept this thought to himself.

'You'll let us know directly you have any news?' said Hartley, as they prepared to take their leave, and Gladwin nodded.

'Yes, I'll ring you up,' he said.

'You'd better come back with me to Harley Street,' said the doctor, as they came out into Whitehall, 'in case anything comes through, it will save time.'

They reached the austere house to find Eric waiting anxiously.

'I wondered what had happened,' he said to his father. 'You said you'd be home, and — '

'I know,' said the doctor, hurriedly, 'but a very serious thing has occurred.'

He told his son what had happened, and Eric's face grew anxious.

'Good Heavens!' he said. 'Can't we do something?'

'That's what I feel,' grunted Jack.

'It seems awful to sit here like this, just waiting while Jill may be — may be . . . ' His voice began husky and choked the end of the sentence.

'There's nothing we can do at the moment,' said Hartley. 'It's useless expending energy, which may be valuable later on, in running about London without a definite objective.'

He went over to the sideboard, poured out a stiff whisky and brought it over to

Jack. 'Drink this,' he said. 'It will pull you together.'

Mallory gulped down the neat spirit and gave him back the glass,

Neither of them made much of the meal, which Wilson presently served and it was cleared away almost untouched. The rest of the evening was spent in gloomy silence, Jack alternating between a furious pacing of the room and a fit of staring hopelessly into the fire. At eleven o'clock the telephone bell rang and Hartley's pulses leaped as he heard Gladwin's voice on the wire, but the inspector had only failure to report.

Up to then, no trace of the taxi or the driver had been found.

'And I don't suppose he ever will be,' muttered Jack pessimistically. 'Li-Sin's won this time, Hartley. He's got her and we shall never see her again.' His voice broke into a sob and he covered his face with his hands.

'Listen,' said the doctor sharply. 'You're doing no good by letting yourself get in that state, Mallory. Pull yourself together and hope for the best.'

151

It was the only comfort he could offer, for in his own heart there was a despair that he felt was difficult to fight.

At twelve o'clock Jack announced his intention of going home, and although Hartley tried to dissuade him and suggested that he should stay the night, the young man was adamant.

'No, I'll go,' he said.

The night was fine and he elected to walk, the cool air might do something to soothe his feverish head. His thoughts were chaotic, wild schemes flowed through his brain, only to be rejected almost as quickly as they were born. He tried to force himself to think clearly, to evolve some practical scheme that might be possible for finding Jill, but it was like trying to break down a brick wall with a feather. There wasn't any practical scheme, from the time she had left the store in Oxford Street she had vanished, and at that moment she might be anywhere. He wasn't even certain that she was still in London and the passing of time only added to the distance that might separate them. There was no hope; no hope at all. It was unlikely that Li-Sin would delay his vengeance, even at that moment he might be putting into effect some ghastly form of torture.

Jack shuddered, it was horrible, too horrible to contemplate, and yet he couldn't shut it out of his mind.

He was passing through a dark street, taking a short cut which would bring him out eventually to Piccadilly, near the block of flats in which he lived, when a closed car that had been trailing him slowly ever since he had left Hartley's, increased its speed and passed him. It drew into the kerb, stopped, and as he came level a muffled figure leaned out of the driving seat and accosted him.

'Excuse me, sir,' said a soft voice, 'but could you tell me how I get to Marble Arch from here?'

Jack stopped impatiently.

'I — ' he began. The rest of his words were smothered as something enveloped his head. He gave a strangled cry and fought desperately to tear the heavy folds of the blanket from his face, but it was reeking with some pungent drug and his efforts were feeble. Just as his knees gave way under him he was hauled into the back of the car, the door slammed shut, and it glided swiftly away from the kerb into the darkness of the night!

15

Jill Tries to Escape

For several minutes after Li-Sin had gone Jill remained quietly in the bunk. It would never do to hurry matters, she must be patient, there was always the possibility that Li-Sin might come back, and so she lay listening and waiting.

Half an hour had passed by her little wristwatch before she decided to start action. Getting up she went softly across to the panel, there was no sound. She knelt down and examined the floor where the Chinaman's foot had pressed. Almost invisible in the boarding she saw a small brass stud, that was raised the eighth of an inch above the level of the floor. She pressed it with her fingers and without a sound the panel swung open.

Beyond was a narrow passageway, and she crept cautiously out, pausing again to look. The lap of water came to her ears, but beyond that, no sound. She made her way stealthily along the passage and presently came to the foot of a ladder, which led up, apparently to open air, for she saw above her the dark vault of the sky, and a star.

For a moment she stood at the foot of the ladder making up her mind what she should do. She had no idea of her whereabouts beyond the fact that she was on some kind of boat that was moored somewhere on the river.

She began to creep up the ladder and cautiously emerged on to a flat deck and then, to her surprise she discovered that she was on a barge, one of those huge, coal bearing barges that are so common on the Thames, and this one was loaded with coal, she could see the lumps of it glistening faintly in the light of the lantern that swung on the stubby mast. But the coal was only a disguise, a thin covering that concealed the real purpose to which the barge was put.

Anyone looking at it from the river would be under the impression that the whole well of the boat was full, whereas below the scattering of heaped coal were luxuriant cabins. This was Li-Sin's chief hideout. She was on the point of stepping out on to the deck when she saw a dim figure standing against the side peering at the water, and very hastily she slid back down the ladder, out of sight.

She must go warily; at the present moment she had the advantage of her enemies for Li-sin was under the impression that she was lying in the cabin in a drugged sleep.

Standing at the foot of the ladder, her ears strained to catch the slightest sound of anyone approaching, she thought rapidly. What was the best thing to be done? If she attempted to escape and was caught they might move her somewhere else. Her wisest plan would be to try and get in touch with the police, but how could this be done? The hoot of a passing tug came to her ears and the barge rocked in the wash as it went by, the sound suggested an idea.

She slipped back along the passage to the cabin she had left, closed the panel, and opening her bag took out a pencil and a notebook. Rapidly she wrote:

Will the person who finds this take it at once to the nearest police station. I am being detained a prisoner on a barge somewhere on the river. The barge looks like an ordinary coal barge but this is a fake. Please communicate with Dr. Hartley, 22a Harley Street, at once.
JILL MALLORY

She read the note through, turned the cigarettes out of the cigarette case and put the paper inside. Opening the panel once more she made her way along the passage and ascended the ladder. The figure that had been leaning over the side had gone and she risked emerging on to the deck.

Across the river she could see one or two twinkling lights, and looking the other way discovered the barge was moored some distance from the shore. She had no idea which part of the river this was, but what she hoped and prayed for now was that another tug should pass.

She had to wait some time and the waiting proved a strain for her nerves. At any moment she expected someone to leap on her out of the shadows and drag her back to the silk-hung cabin before she could put her plan into execution.

But not a sign of life stirred, the barge might have been deserted for any evidence there was of any living soul on board.

Presently she heard the thud, thud of engines and saw a tug chugging its way towards her. Now was her opportunity.

She waited until the lumbering craft was level with the barge and then, with all the strength of her arm she flung the cigarette case towards it. If it fell short her plan was a failure, but it didn't. By some miracle she had judged her distance well and she heard the clatter of the case as it struck metal. Somebody uttered an exclamation that came faintly to her across the water and then, turning, she stumbled down the ladder, hurried back along the passage and reaching the cabin shut the panel with a trembling hand.

She had succeeded! With any luck, that

message would be in the hands of the police in a few hours, and they would notify Hartley. The people on the tug would be able to say at what point of the river it had reached them and the police would institute a search. There was every chance that she might be rescued in time.

She lay back on the bunk, feeling almost contented. She must have fallen asleep, for she remembered nothing more until she awakened with a start to hear the sound of shuffling footsteps approaching the panel in the wall. Through half closed eyes she watched it. Presently it opened. Two Chinamen came in, carrying a limp form between them. From outside in the passage she heard the voice of Li-Sin. He was speaking in Chinese and she couldn't understand what he said. The two Chinamen laid their burden down and, turning, went out. The tall, thin figure in the silken robe appeared for a moment in the oblong opening and stared down at the motionless form on the floor, then raising his eyes he looked across to the bunk. Jill lay motionless, and apparently he was satisfied, for without a word he went out and the panel closed.

She waited a moment or two and then slipping from the bunk she rapidly crossed the floor and looked down at the man they had brought in. It took all her willpower to reject the cry that rose in her throat, for the unconscious man that lay at her feet was her husband!

16

The Yard Takes Action

Dr. Hartley spent a restless and wakeful night. In spite of his good advice to Jack Mallory to keep cool, it was difficult to follow it himself. The thought of going to bed was intolerable, and he spent the night in his study, trying vainly to formulate some plan of action. At eight o'clock, tired and weary, he telephoned to the Mallorys' flat and here a shock awaited him, for the maid who answered the phone informed him that Mr. Mallory had not come home!

Hartley hung up the receiver with despair in his heart. It could only mean one thing, that Li-Sin had got Jack Mallory too. The young man must have been spirited away during his journey from Harley Street to Piccadilly.

He ordered some coffee and some toast and when he had consumed a light meal he set off for Scotland Yard. It was nine o'clock when he arrived and Inspector Gladwin was glancing through his morning mail.

'Hello, Doctor,' he greeted. 'Any news?'

Hartley nodded.

'Yes, bad news,' he said. 'They've got Mallory as well.'

The inspector looked concerned.

'How do you know that?' he asked.

Hartley explained.

'H'm,' muttered Gladwin. 'Well, we've heard nothing about that taxi driver, and until we do, or get hold of some other kind of clue, we're helpless.'

'I know,' said the doctor. 'That's the maddening part of it, we can do nothing! Nothing! This fiend has beaten us, Gladwin. He killed Sir Edward and he's got Mallory and his wife in his clutches. I suppose I shall be the next to go, and if I do, you're helpless.'

'We can take precautions against your going,' said Gladwin. 'I'll have you put under police protection from this moment.'

The telephone at his elbow rang and he

picked up the receiver.

'Hello? Oh, yes.' Hartley saw his face change as he reached for a pencil and began scribbling on a pad by his side. 'I'll come along at once,' he said. 'Keep the man until I get there.' He slammed the receiver back on its hook and turned to the doctor. 'That was the Wanstead River Police Station,' he said. 'The skipper of a tug called there half an hour ago and told the inspector in charge a strange story. He said he'd been passing Wanstead Flats early this morning in his tug when something had clattered on the deck. One of his men had picked it up and brought it to him. It was a thin, platinum cigarette case, and inside was a note signed 'Jill Mallory'.'

Hartley uttered an exclamation, his face eager.

'What did the note say?' he asked quickly.

'The note said that she was detained a prisoner on a coal barge,' answered Gladwin, 'and would the finder of the message take it to the nearest police station, and communicate with you. The inspector at Wanstead thought it was better to ring up the Yard first.'

Hartley sprang to his feet.

'We'd better get there at once,' he said. 'We may be in time yet.'

'I'll order a police car,' said Gladwin, at once reaching for the 'phone.

Five minutes later they were seated in the long car speeding towards Wanstead.

In the little river police station they found Inspector Bristow talking to a thickset man whose appearance stamped his occupation.

'This is Mr. Tom Gunn, sir,' he said, addressing Gladwin. 'He's the fellow who found the message.'

Mr. Gunn grinned.

'I thought it was rummy,' he said. 'Cigarette cases don't drop out of the sky.'

'Can you tell us the place where the case was thrown on to your boat?' asked Gladwin.

The skipper nodded.

'Yes,' he replied. 'It were just opposite the A.B.L. engineering works, there's a mooring place for barges there, 'bout 'alf a dozen of them there are, and this cigarette case must have been thrown from one of those.'

Gladwin turned to Bristowe.

'How many men can you get together?' he asked quickly.

The inspector of the river police wrinkled his brows.

'Twenty,' he said.

'Get them,' ordered Gladwin shortly, 'and a fast police launch. And get them as quickly as you can!'

The inspector jerked the telephone towards him and began issuing orders.

It was half an hour, however, before the reserves could be mustered, and another quarter before they were all seated in the long police boat that came gliding up to the steps of the station.

'You come with us,' said Gladwin to Gunn, 'and show us the place.'

With a grin of delight the skipper obeyed.

'What's it all about?' he asked.

'It's a very serious business,' said the inspector. 'That message you received came from a lady who is being held a prisoner by a Chinese gang.'

'Blimey!' exclaimed Mr. Gunn disgustedly. 'I reckon I wouldn't mind havin' a go at them.'

The police boat shot away from the landing stage and headed down river. The morning was cold, with a driving drizzle of rain and the sombre scenery of the river added to the depression that had settled over the party. The boat moved swiftly, its sharp prow cleaving the oily grey water that broke on each side in a white-topped wave.

They had been moving steadily for half an hour when Mr. Gunn suddenly pointed.

'There y'are,' he said. 'That's the place.'

Gladwin followed the direction of his upraised arm and saw half a dozen barges moored some distance from the melancholy waste of the flats. He gave an order to the man at the wheel.

'Make for the opposite bank and stop,' he said.

The police launch veered, shot over to the shadow of a crazy wharf and slowed.

'Now, the question is,' muttered the inspector, 'which of those barges is the one we want?'

He stared at the huge boats, his brows drawn together, in a frown. There was not much to choose between them, they were all coal barges and so far as he could see they were all fully laden. It seemed difficult to imagine there could be anyone on board any of them, for there was no sign of a living soul, and the coal, apparently, completely filled them.

'You've no idea, I suppose, which one that cigarette case was thrown from?' he asked, and Mr. Gunn shook his head.

'No, I can't tell you that, mate,' he replied. 'I only knows it must 'ave been from one of them, 'cause there was no other craft near my boat at the time, and it would 'ave been impossible for anyone to 'ave thrown it so far if they'd been standing on the bank.'

Gladwin was silent for a moment.

'H'm,' he said at last. 'Well, I suppose we shall have to try them all. Take us over there, will you?'

The man at the wheel nodded, pulled a

lever and the police boat shot forward again. It came round in a wide sweep and drew in close to the barges. Standing up in the bows Gladwin gave a stentorian shout.

'Ahoy, there,' he called. 'Anyone on board?'

Dead silence answered him. After waiting a moment he shouted again, but still there was no reply. The barges were silent and deserted.

⋆   ⋆   ⋆

Jill gazed down at the unconscious figure of her husband and her heart beat faster. He was alive, for that she was thankful, but he was breathing heavily, and obviously under the influence of some drug. She chafed him and called his name but she might as well have been speaking to a log for all the answer she got. Kneeling down beside him she loosened his collar and she was so occupied with this that she failed to hear the panel silently open, and was unaware that Li-Sin had returned until he spoke.

'So!' he said, in his soft guttural tone, 'you have recovered consciousness, Mrs. Mallory?'

She looked up, startled, full into the black, almond-shaped eyes that were gazing steadily at her.

'Yes, I've recovered consciousness,' she answered steadily. 'I see that you have succeeded in kidnapping my husband, too.'

Li-Sin inclined his head.

'The gods have been kind to me,' he said simply. 'Today will see the second part of my revenge complete.'

'What do you intend to do with us?' she asked.

He closed the panel behind him, and came a few steps further into the cabin.

'I propose to exact vengeance for the desecration of the temple Tsao-Sun. Vengeance against the destroyer of the sacred Idol.' He gave his habitual little jerky bow. 'It was your husband, Mrs. Mallory, who stole the Idol from its rightful home. But for him it would remain in the temple now, it would not have been handled by infidel hands, and eventually destroyed.'

She remained silent, for there was truth in this tall Chinaman's statement. Although Jack had acted with the intention of retrieving the family's fortune he had no right to do what he had done.

'What do you intend to do with us?' she asked again.

'In good time you will see,' said Li-Sin. 'I have evolved a plan which will satisfy the judgment of the gods. You, yourself, will remain unharmed, but for the rest of your life you will be a broken woman. Your husband will die and it will be by your hand that death will come to him!'

She looked at him in amazement.

'You're mad!' she said. 'Do you suppose for an instant that you could force me to kill my husband?'

'I not only suppose,' he answered, 'but I know.'

From beneath his robe he took out a small, crystal flask. She saw that it contained a few drops of a bright green fluid. He held it up, turning it this way and that in his thin, yellow fingers.

'I have here,' he said, 'a drug that is

unknown to your Western science. It has peculiar properties. An injection produces the effect of completely paralysing the will; although the person so injected is perfectly conscious and aware of what they are doing, they are so powerless to assert their own will that any suggestion offered to them they have to act upon. There is no need for me to explain further, I'm sure you have gathered my meaning.'

She had, and the horror which overwhelmed her made her feel physically sick, and her voice, when she spoke, was husky and totally unlike her own.

'You — you wouldn't do such a horrible thing?' she whispered.

Li-Sin's face was expressionless.

'I would, and I shall,' he answered.

He replaced the little bottle from where he had taken it, beneath his robe and pressed on the spring operating the panel.

'In two hours it will be time,' he said. 'At the end of that period I shall return.'

He slipped through the oblong opening and the panel closed behind him. A wave of panic swept over the girl, that inexorable voice had filled her with terror. She knew he had been speaking the truth, unless something happened between now and his return, hers would be the hand to strike Jack's deathblow. It was horrible, a fiendish scheme. Infinitely more dreadful than any form of torture he could have devised. For the rest of her life she would go through a living hell, knowing that she had killed her husband.

She felt her brain reeling at the horror of the thought, but by a gigantic effort she managed to calm herself. It was no good giving way, something was bound to happen, this monstrous thing could never be allowed to take place. Perhaps the message she had thrown on the passing tug would reach Hartley in time. Perhaps even now they were hurrying to her rescue.

Mechanically she lit one of her cigarettes and paced up and down, smoking jerkily. The tobacco soothed her strained nerves. Perhaps Li-Sin was bluffing, perhaps he had told her what he had in order to terrify her, and perpetrate a subtle form of torture.

She paused and looked down at the still unconscious form of Jack. His face was peaceful, and he might merely have been asleep. He looked terribly young, it was outrageous that he should die. She wondered if it was any good attempting to escape, but the thought had barely entered her mind before she rejected it.

If there had been any chance of that Li-Sin would not have left her free. She guessed that the passage way beyond the panel was being watched and in any case it would be beyond her to move Jack in his present state.

The time passed slowly. She looked at her little wristwatch and to her surprise saw that it was eight o'clock. It must be light outside.

Jack stirred restlessly and groaned. She was by his side instantly and as she bent down over him his eyelids flickered, the effects of the drug were evidently wearing off. Better, she thought despairingly, if it had not. If it was willed that he should die, it was better he should die without recovering consciousness, than to know that it was her hand that sent him into the unknown!

He opened his eyes and stared up, wildly, and then a puzzled expression crept into them as he saw Jill.

'Jill,' he murmured feebly. 'Where — where am I?'

She pillowed his head on her lap.

'It's all right, darling,' she said soothingly. 'You're with me.'

For a moment he lay still contentedly, and then he frowned and tried to struggle up.

'But — but?' he whispered hoarsely. 'This is not our flat. What is this place?'

She saw that his memory was coming back as his face changed, and the look of puzzled bewilderment was replaced by one of horror.

'My God!' he said. 'I remember. You disappeared and I was attacked on my way home from Hartley's. That devil's got us!'

Before she could answer a gong rang brazenly from somewhere close at hand. Its vibrating strokes had scarcely died to silence before there was a click, and the panel opened and Li-Sin came in. He was followed by two Chinamen, and in his hand he carried a long, lacquered object, of apparently great age.

'The time has come, Mrs. Mallory,' he said, as one of the men closed the panel behind him. 'And as I expected, your husband has regained his senses. That is well. That is what I was waiting for. It would have been a pity to have enacted our little drama without his being able to share in its enjoyment.'

'You damned beast!' gasped Jack. 'What are you going to do?'

'You will see, Mr. Mallory,' said Li-Sin imperturbably. 'Your wife already knows.'

He uttered a sharp order in Chinese and the two men with him sprang forward and gripped Jill by the arms. Jack gave a strangled cry of rage.

'Call those brutes off,' he said hoarsely, and tried to struggle to his feet, but although his mind was clear and he could move a little his limbs were heavy and partially paralysed.

'It is useless attempting to try and get up, Mr. Mallory,' said Li-Sin soothingly.

'The drug that has been administered to you renders it, I assure you, impossible.'

He laid down the lacquered object that he had carried in his hand reverently and withdrew from beneath his robe a silver hypodermic. Holding it delicately in his hand he advanced towards the struggling Jill. The men who were holding her possessed colossal strength, and although she tried to break away she was helpless in their grip.

'It is useless struggling against the inevitable,' said Li-Sin, and pinching up a ridge of flesh on one of her arms he inserted the needle and pressed the plunger home.

She screamed and Jack swore, Li-Sin stepped back.

'So,' he said, 'in five minutes the gift of free will shall have been taken from you.'

She felt a coldness creeping through her veins. Miraculously it mounted until it engulfed her brain. Nothing seemed to matter, nothing!

Li-Sin watched her, his lined yellow face impassive. The coldness seemed to be drawing all her strength, she could no longer think clearly, although her mind was by no means dull. She could see and understand.

'Loose her!' ordered the tall Chinaman, and the two men who had been holding her stepped aside. 'You hear me?' continued Li-Sin. 'Nod your head.'

Jill nodded.

'You are conscious, but whatever I ask you, you must obey. Walk over to the bunk.'

Like an automaton she walked over.

'Now come back,' he ordered, and she came back.

'My God!' cried Jack. 'You damned fiend. What have you done to her?'

'You will see, Mr. Mallory,' said Li-Sin, smoothly, and turning he picked up the long, lacquered object which he had brought in with him. 'This,' he said, 'is the sacred sword of Tu-Lin. It has been in my family for generations. It belonged to my ancestors and their ancestors before them, and yet it is as sharp today as when it was originally forged.'

He drew from the lacquered scabbard a keen flashing blade. Presenting the hilt to

Jill he ordered her to take it. She stretched out a hand and her fingers closed round the hilt.

'At this moment,' he said, 'the gods have conferred upon you a great honour. They have decreed that your hand shall be the hand to avenge the sacred Idol of Tsao-Sun. The desecrator of the temple lies before you. Strike and carry out the vengeance of Li-Sin!'

Jack's eyes glared in horror as Jill stepped forward, the sword clutched in both her hands. For a moment a tremor went through her and then slowly she raised the blade above her head!

17

The Chase

The upraised sword was quivering in her hand. It had begun its descending stroke when from somewhere outside came a stentorian shout.

'Ahoy, there!' called a gruff voice. 'Is anyone aboard?'

Li-Sin's breath escaped from between his lips in a hissing exhalation.

'Stop!' he whispered, and obeying, Jill checked the descending blade.

'That's Gladwin,' muttered Jack. 'Thank God the police have arrived!'

'But they have arrived too late,' hissed the Chinaman, his face convulsed in fury. 'I will not be baulked of my revenge. Strike!' he cried.

Obedient to his command Jill raised the sword again, but in his excitement Li-Sin had stepped too near to the prone figure of Mallory on the floor. The young man shot out his hand and gripped the Chinaman by his ankles. A jerk and he went over, and in falling cannoned into thc girl The descending sword came down, a foot away from Jack's head, and bit into the woodwork of the floor, cleaving the thick carpet like a hot wire through cheese.

'This way, Gladwin,' shouted Jack, and then the two Chinamen who had been momentarily paralysed sprang at him, one of them clapping his hand over his mouth, but Jack's shout had been heard.

A dull murmur of excited voices came to him from outside and then the scraping sound of feet against the side of the barge. A few seconds later they heard the sound of heavy footsteps on the deck above and Gladwin's voice shouting again.

Li-Sin got quickly to his feet. With a panther-like spring he reached the panel, stamped on the floor and it swung open. As he emerged into the passage Gladwin came stumbling down the ladder at the other end. He caught sight of the Chinaman and his hand went up, holding the automatic, but Li-Sin had slipped out of his enveloping robe, and as the inspector levelled the weapon he flung the heavy silk robe full at him. It enveloped Gladwin's head and pistol arm and before he could extricate himself from its folds Li-Sin had stepped past him and was up the ladder.

A glance showed him that the deck of the barge was alive with policemen. He made a leap for the side and dived cleanly into the water. Hartley saw him go and shouted.

'There he is! After him!'

He sprang from the barge back into the launch, two of the policemen with him. They saw the black head of the Chinaman, a dancing dot on the water, swimming strongly towards a long graceful speedboat that was moored near the bank. As the man in charge of the police boat started his engine the Chinaman reached his objective and pulled himself aboard. With incredible swiftness he cast off and they heard the rhythmic hum of a motor engine.

'After him!' cried Hartley. 'If you are

not careful he'll get away yet!'

The police launch put on speed, but Li-Sin's boat had already left the bank. It went streaking down the river, its heavy wash trailing out behind it. The man at the wheel of the police launch looked grave.

'It's faster than our boat,' he muttered. 'I doubt if we can catch her.'

He opened his throttle wide and the distance between the two crafts decreased slightly, but it was only for a moment, and then the motorboat containing Li-Sin shot ahead.

Hartley took the automatic pistol from one of the policemen and fired. A spout of water threw up behind the fugitive, and Li-Sin looked round. Hartley fired again, but his bullet went wide, for the Chinaman's boat continued on its way unharmed. The doctor lowered his aim a little and sent a stream of bullets hailing about the propeller, but apparently he failed to hit a vital spot, for the boat kept on, gaining rapidly, and they saw ahead a bank of river mist. Hartley emptied the magazine in a last desperate attempt to check the fleeing launch and gave an exclamation of satisfaction as just before it vanished in the enveloping mist he saw it swerve.

Out of the white vapour came the shrill hoot of a tug's siren.

'I'm afraid we've lost him,' muttered the man at the wheel, and the words had scarcely left his lips when they heard ahead a startled shout and a crash.

'My God! I believe he's collided with the tug,' said Hartley, and as they entered the curtain of fog they saw that he was right.

A big tugboat was drawing to a standstill and on the water round its bows floated the wreckage of Li-Sin's launch. The captain and crew of the tug were leaning over the sides, staring at the water, and Hartley called to them as the driver of the police boat drew alongside. 'Did you smash into a launch?' he asked.

The captain uttered a lurid oath.

'The launch smashed into us,' he bellowed. 'The blamed fool drove straight into our bows!'

They looked about for some sign of

Li-Sin, but there was none. No sign of a human being was visible on the grey expanse of oily water.

★　★　★

'I don't think there can be any doubt that he was drowned,' said Gladwin, later on that evening, as he, Hartley, Eric, Jack, and Jill sat round the fire in the Mallorys' flat. 'Most likely he was struck by the tug and sank immediately.'

Dr. Hartley nodded slowly.

'Let's hope so,' he said.

Neither Jack nor his wife were much the worse for their ordeal of the morning. The drug that Li-Sin had administered to the girl had quickly worn off, and she had felt no ill effects, neither had Jack. Beyond a splitting headache which had quickly worn off he had felt as fit as a fiddle once the paralysing effects had left his limbs.

Until darkness had fallen the river police had dragged that part of the river where the accident had happened, but up to now they had failed to find any trace of the body of the Chinaman. But this was not surprising, for the Thames contains many swift undercurrents, and if it had got in the grip of one of these it might have been carried several miles down the river.

'I should feel more satisfied,' said Hartley, after a long pause, 'if we could find the fellow's body.'

Gladwin shot him a quick glance.

'You don't think he's escaped, do you?' he asked.

The doctor shrugged his shoulders.

'It seems impossible,' he admitted. 'But, well, you never can tell, and I must say that I should feel more relieved if we knew that he was dead.'

Two days later Gladwin rang him up.

'Would you like to come with me to Gravesend?' he said. 'If you're not busy I think you might be interested.'

'Why, what is it?' asked Hartley quickly.

'The body of a Chinaman was taken out of the river this morning,' answered the inspector. 'From the description, and the clothing, I think it must be Li-Sin.'

'I'll come round to the Yard at once,'

said Hartley, and rang off.

He met Gladwin and they motored down to Gravesend. On a marble slab in the little mortuary they were shown the figure of a Chinaman. He had been in the water for so long that it was impossible to recognise his features, but the sodden clothing in which he was clad were the clothes they had last seen Li-Sin wearing.

'I don't think there's any doubt,' said Gladwin, so from henceforward, you and the Mallorys ought to be safe.'

Hartley went back to town with a lighter heart, and that evening he acquainted Jack and Jill with the finding of the body.

'Poor devil!' said the young man. 'It was a shocking end.'

'He deserved it,' said the girl.

'It all depends how you look at these things,' said Hartley. 'After all, there was something to be said for him. He was only acting according to his rights. Wrong from our point of view, but right from his. And he had more to justify him than Jack had when he took that idol from the temple of Tsao-Sun.'

Mallory nodded.

'Yes, I agree with you,' he said. 'My action was theft, pure and simple, and I've never ceased to regret it.'

'Well, let's hope it is all over now,' said Hartley, 'If the body I saw at Gravesend was the body of Li-Sin I don't think we shall be troubled any more.'

'Unless,' said Jack grimly, 'another emissary of the temple sets out to avenge him.'

'Yes, there's always that possibility,' remarked the doctor gravely. 'You stirred up a lot of trouble, young man, and there's no telling where it may end, we'll hope it's ended now.'

The winter merged into spring, and the spring into summer and nothing occurred to mar the tranquillity of the Mallorys' lives. Hartley went down to spend a few weeks with them in June and in the peace of the old house and the surrounding country forgot the exciting events of the winter. And the Mallorys forgot them too, for in the autumn a son was born to Jill, and in the interest of the new arrival the machinations of Li-Sin faded into the forgotten past.

★   ★   ★

In the dimly-lit temple of Tsao-Sun, lighted by the three lamps that were never allowed to go out, a figure made obeisance before the huge idol of Buddha. Kneeling humbly on the gold steps it raised its hands above its head and called down the blessing of the God.

A venerable priest came slowly from an arched doorway and approached the kneeling figure.

'You have returned, my son,' said the old Chinaman.

Li-Sin raised his head.

'I have returned, Oh Father,' he said, 'but who knows how long I shall remain. My mission is unfinished. Until I have completed my task how can I seek the peace and rest?'

'You speak words of wisdom,' said the priest. 'It is written in the book of fate that for twelve moons shall you rest, and then once more set out on your pilgrimage. Oh, blessed Li-Sin, Prince of Tu-Lin, you have been chosen by the Gods to wipe out the accursed race whose fingers defiled the sacred offspring of Buddha. In part of your task you have succeeded, rest oh my son, until such time as the gods shall call upon you to return and complete your work.'

He bowed to the Buddha and passed on into the shadows of the temple, and motionless before the great figure of the god Li-Sin knelt in prayer.

THE END

We do hope that you have enjoyed reading this large print book.

Did you know that all of our titles are available for purchase?

We publish a wide range of high quality large print books including:
Romances, Mysteries, Classics
General Fiction
Non Fiction and Westerns

Special interest titles available in large print are:
The Little Oxford Dictionary
Music Book, Song Book
Hymn Book, Service Book

Also available from us courtesy of Oxford University Press:
Young Readers' Dictionary
(large print edition)
Young Readers' Thesaurus
(large print edition)

For further information or a free brochure, please contact us at:
Ulverscroft Large Print Books Ltd.,
The Green, Bradgate Road, Anstey,
Leicester, LE7 7FU, England.
Tel: (00 44) **0116 236 4325**
Fax: (00 44) **0116 234 0205**

*Other titles in the
Linford Mystery Library:*

ECHO OF BARBARA

John Burke

Imprisoned for ten years, Sam West-wood had clung on by remembering his daughter Barbara. Now released, his main desire was to see her. However, Barbara detested her father's memory, and leaving her mother and her brother Roger at home, she had walked out and could not be found. But Roger had his own reason for wanting Barbara back: a wild scheme which, with the addition of Sam's old associates, would prove to have dangerous complications . . .

THE FACELESS ONES

Gerald Verner

An organisation which was so mysterious and vast, its people had been called 'The Faceless Ones'; their file, held by the British Security Service, was labelled 'Group X'. So who are these people — what are their intentions? Magda Vettrilli had found out, but before she could pass on her knowledge, she was shot on the steps of the British Consulate in Tangier. Egerton Scott must discover their identity, and the objective behind 'Group X'. But can he succeed?

THE PURPLE PLAGUE

Derwent Steele

The first victim was a shopkeeper in Bradford. A week later, a publican in Newcastle had collapsed into a coma and later died. Inexorably, similar deaths followed, all in different parts of the country. It appeared that a new form of bacillus was involved. Where had it originated from, how had it arrived into the country, and why did it occur in such diverse places? Dubbed by the press as the 'Purple Plague', was the disease natural? *Or man-made . . . ?*